RAT'S NEST

Also by Charles West

Funnelweb

RAT'S NEST

Charles West

Walker and Company
New York

First published in the United States of America in 1990
by Walker Publishing Company, Inc.

Previously published as The Destruction Man, 1976.
Published in Great Britain, by Robert Hale & Company,
Clarkenwell House, Clarkenwell Green, London.

Published simultaneously in Canada by Thomas Allen & Son
Canada, Limited, Markham, Ontario

Library of Congress Cataloging-in-Publication Data

West, Charles.
Rat's nest / Charles West.
Rev. ed. of: The destruction man. 1976.
ISBN 0-8027-5765-0
I. West, Charles. Destruction man.   II. Title.
PR6073.E7624R3   1990
823'.914—dc20   90-31099

Printed in the United States of America

2   4   6   8   10   9   7   5   3   1

Chapter One

'Bloody Judas!' Mick's beefy moon-face was fiery-red, and drops of sweat beaded his eyebrows. 'What in the name of all the holy bloody saints d'ye think you're doin'?'

'It's a Demo,' I said. 'A protest against the needless destruction of this theatre.' There were fifteen of us; ten actresses, three schoolteachers, an assistant librarian and me. We carried placards, with hand-painted slogans; mine said SAVE THIS FINE OLD THEATRE. Punchy, without being inflammatory, I thought.

Mick hopped about on the tips of his toes, like an operatic tenor straining for an impossibly high note. 'You brainless fart!' he yelled. 'D'you know who has the contract to pull down this ould ruin?'

'You're going to tell me that you have. But it doesn't make any difference.'

One of the teachers said, 'This will be the third theatre in Sydney to be demolished within three years. Somebody had to show some concern.'

Mick withered her with a bloodshot glance. 'Missus, if everybody in this territory showed their true concern for this dump, you'ld hear the yawn from here to Connemara. This haybarn hasn't seen a live show since Queen Victoria's Jubilee. Last four years, it's been a Furniture Suppository.' Mick had a fine Irish disregard for the trivial proprieties of the English language. 'As for you, you useless bloody gurrier,' he snarled, turning his attention back to me, 'I wouldn't sullify me tongue trying to put a name to you.

5

You're fired!' He stamped away into the echoing, lavatory-tiled foyer of the building we were picketing to protect.

Fourteen pairs of eyes regarded me critically. Since my fellow-demonstrators were all female, and the tallest of them hardly reached to my shoulder, I felt as conspicuous as a sunflower on a bowling-green.

'Who was that gentleman?' The assistant librarian voiced the general curiosity.

'My employer.' I reconsidered that. 'My ex-employer.'

One of the actresses registered heavy suspicion. 'But wasn't that Mick Dooley, the demolition contractor?'

'It was.'

' "Dooley The Destroyer"?'

'That's right.'

'And you work for him?'

'Not at the moment. He's just fired me.' I might have added that he fired me on average once a fortnight, but they looked confused enough already.

The Cause was momentarily forgotten. A big-nosed blonde took up the inquisition. 'You mean you earn your living—?'

'That's right. I knock buildings down. With a hammer.'

'But?—why?'

'It's better money than pushing a cab. And you don't get lost so often.'

'How peculiar!' The assistant librarian was obviously having second thoughts about the social status of this particular Demo. 'I mean—you appeared to be quite a gentleman.'

'Thank you.'

'Are you making fun of us?' someone asked.

'No. I happen to agree with you that too many theatres are being pulled down in this city. Someone ought to protest.'

'You don't sound like an Australian.' The schoolteacher made it an accusation.

'I'm not.'

6

'You sound like an American.'

'I suppose I do, but I'm not that, either.'

They had run out of questions. They shuffled their feet and frowned meaningfully at each other. I had offended them in some way, but they couldn't quite define the offence.

'Do you think we're doing any good?' the youngest actress whimpered to no-one in particular. 'Nobody seems very interested.'

She was not over-stating the case. Our total audience consisted of one apathetic policeman, and a sandwich-board man advertising the Christmas Fair at a department store. Because of the heat, the sandwich-board man had taken off his shirt. From where I stood, he seemed to be wearing nothing but his boards and a pair of sandals.

It was not yet nine-thirty in the morning, but already the street was as hot as an oven. The city was in the grip of a heat-wave that looked like going on forever. The nights were only fractionally cooler than the days; and every morning, the down-town jungle of concrete and steel still throbbed with heat from the previous day's sunshine. The Protest Meeting began to wilt.

'I do believe,' the youngest actress murmured anxiously, 'that my nose is starting to peel.'

A concerted shudder ran through the group. As if on a pre-arranged signal, the meeting began to break up. The Protest had been made; it was not our fault if nothing had been achieved. And, as someone thoughtfully observed, the day could be more usefully spent doing Christmas shopping in some air-conditioned department store. I propped my board against a glass-panelled door, and nodded my farewells as they twittered off. Someone shouted 'Merry Christmas,' and they all giggled like school-girls.

The day had started badly. But I couldn't have known then, that it was going to turn into the worst day of my life.

The sensible thing to do, was to go home and take some beer out of the refrigerator. Instead, I chose to wander round the city street, depressing myself. The sun beat down mercilessly on shop-fronts strung with Christmas decorations, its glare mocking the plastic holly and the cotton-wool snow. Sweating mothers with sunburnt children beamed fatuously as 'Jingle Bells' blared out from loud-speakers in shop doorways. A freckled Santa Claus in the last stages of heat exhaustion gulped Coca-Cola furtively through his nylon beard. In a side-road off George Street, a demolition company—not Mick's—was knocking down a hideous old church, enveloped stiflingly in its own cloud of grey dust.

I went down to the Harbour, and rode the Manly ferry, for something to do. The boat scooped up a faint trickle of cool air from the sapphire-and-diamond surface of the water, to temper the heady exhaust fumes from its own engines. On the round trip, my fellow passengers dropped fifty-three empty beer cans and a few bottles over the starboard rail. I didn't attempt to keep a tally on the port side.

The day crawled by somehow.

I arrived at Helen's office just before five. The agency where she worked was as aggressively modern as this week's Colour Supplement. It had a waiting-room with bulbous furniture like plastic balloons, and treacherous shin-high tables crowded with expensive art-books. The air-conditioning struck at the skin like the wind off the Arctic tundra.

I pressed the buzzer, and Helen came out of her office. She looked as always, perfect: cool, neat, self-possessed, utterly desirable, from her slim ankles to her darkly-shining hair. She came swiftly into my arms; her lips were cool and soft and sweet. The sharp tang of her favourite perfume made my senses reel. She looked up enquiringly into my face. 'Lover?'

'Mm?'

'You look a bit grim?'

'I've been thinking.'

'It seems to have been a strain.'

'It was.' I told her about my day, realizing, as the words tumbled out, that I had been saving them up for this moment.

She shook her head. 'That's not it; that's not any of it. You've been sacked before, and this certainly isn't the first time you've worked yourself into a lather about how stupid and self-destructive people are. You've even written verse about it. This is something else; something much worse.'

'I guess you're right. I want to marry you.'

She stood very still, her face stricken. 'Marriage?'

'Very bourgeois and reactionary of me, I admit. But it's what I want.'

'But—why? What can you possibly want of me that you haven't already got? I love you: you know you can have me at the drop of an eyelid, virtually any time of the day or night. I thought you were happy with things as they are.'

'I thought so too. But apparently I was wrong.'

Her eyes were wide and dark, and there was a pinched look about her face. I recognized the symptoms. We were in for a blazing row.

'How long have we known each other?' she demanded.

'Five months. Long enough.'

'And we've been lovers since—when? Our third meeting?' She was testing me. 'Second,' I said smugly.

'And in all that time, have I ever been niggardly in bed?'

'You have always been perfect.'

'Have I ever been jealous, prying, sulky, over-possessive or nagging?'

'No.'

'And you want me to start *now*?'

I thought about it. Seriously. 'Yes.'

'*Why*, for God's sake? You know nothing about me.'

'I know everything about you. You're crazy about music,

9

food, drink, clothes, sunbathing, Flemish painting, old films and everything the Lancôme Company ever made. You hate newspapers, cheap soap, plastic flowers and dirty jokes. You haven't read a novel for ten years. You are unique, and I love you.'

She said a little breathlessly, 'That's no basis for marriage.'

'Why not?'

'Oh, I don't know!' She moved away from me and stood by the window, amusement and exasperation mingling in her face. She looked for a moment as if she might burst into tears. Outside, the shadows were lengthening, but the air still shimmered in the nagging heat. In the street below, people moved listlessly, like fish in stale water. Soon, the rush-hour traffic would build up to plague proportions, adding its ill-tempered quota of noise and stink.

Helen said blankly, 'What's wrong with what we have?'

'Nothing. It's perfect. In fact, its too goddam perfect. I'd believe in it a lot more if it were more human.'

'Messier, you mean.'

'Yes.'

'I didn't realize you were so old-fashioned.'

I shrugged my shoulders in defeat. It just wasn't my day. 'I'm sorry. Forget it.'

'You don't have to apologize,' she said softly. 'I'm old-fashioned, too. But I can't marry you. Not yet, anyway.'

'Why not?'

She looked prim and delicious, 'Because—no, keep your distance—because, in spite of your apparent intelligence and undeniable virility and other charms, visible and invisible, you're a mess.'

'Reform me.'

'No, I'm being serious. You're free, you've got money, you've even published two rather meagre volumes of verse—' I winced, to let her know she was on target, and she hammered on—'Oh, I know they were well received, but where's the next one? Since your mother died, you've just bummed around the world, as aimless and unambitious as a neutered dormouse. You know, and I know, that you're not going to work on a demolition gang all your life—and what a Freudian choice of occupation that is!—but for the present you're content to drift, and wait for Shangri-La to show up on the starboard bow. No, you're fine and romantic right now—I'm not complaining on that score—but until you can make up your mind about life, I don't think you can make up your mind about marriage. I don't want to be on the receiving end of one of your mistakes.'

I gloomed out of the window. The rejection was bad enough, but the character analysis that went with it was a bouquet of nettles. I could think of nothing to say.

Across the street, an ice-cream van had broken down, its bonnet propped open as a distress signal. It stood in glaring sunshine, only a few yards short of the nearest shade, but the driver obviously hadn't the energy to shift it. He was slumped low behind the wheel, reading a comic paper. The traffic noise from the nearby main road gradually increased in volume. An empty truck racketed past, belching clouds of black smoke, which hung knee-high in the sluggish air. A girl, dressed in a sloppy green frock and a wide-brimmed straw hat, stared into a shop window full of office furniture.

'You're the nearest I'll ever get to Shangri-La,' I said at last. 'I was hoping you would come back to Boston with me.'

'You didn't tell me you were leaving?'

'I didn't decide until this afternoon. I did a lot of thinking today, and eventually arrived at the conclusion you must have reached months ago. You're right—it's time I stopped drifting. It's time I went back.'

'To Boston?'

'Not just that. I want to start work again. Finish that lousy thesis. Maybe start playing with words again.'

'Then why the hell didn't you say so at first, instead of letting me rave on about your wasted young life?' Her cheeks were scarlet and her eyes glistened with tears. She fumbled for a handkerchief and flapped her hands angrily when she couldn't find one. She ran to her office, and paused in the doorway, not looking at me. 'Don't go away. I've got some poise-recovering to do. And don't say another word, or I'll brain you!'

She was gone for some time. There was more activity on the street now, as the clerks and typists and grey-suited executives came out of the office buildings, flinching as they stepped into the brutal heat. The ice-cream van still stood by the kerb, its glass sides tightly shuttered. The girl in the green dress walked a few paces, turned, and went on staring into the shop window. She had the splayed bird-walk and the muscular calf development of the professional dancer. The stream of pedestrians broke and flowed round her, an obstacle in the current.

Helen came out at last. She had changed into a yellow linen dress which was a perfect foil for the silky tan of her skin. 'What do you think?' she smiled. 'Approve?'

'It's new?'

'Yes indeed. It's my engagement dress, I think. That is, if you're going to ask me again.'

'Marry me.'

'You bet!' She walked towards me with provocative grace, and wound her arms about my neck. 'Let's go home and celebrate, lover. Afterwards, you can take me out to an enormous and expensive meal, then we'll go home and celebrate again.'

'Home?'

'Your place, my place, it doesn't matter so long as there's a bed. From now on, where you are is home, my darling. Now brace yourself for an engagement kiss.'

She certainly had a sense of occasion. Her kiss made my knees buckle. She detached herself breathlessly from my arms. 'Come on, take me home. Time's a-wasting.' She moved to pick up her handbag, then paused, staring out of the window. Someone in the home-going crowd had bumped into the girl in the green frock, and knocked her hat off. Her hair shone like metal in the sunlight: a sleek cap of platinum blonde, dragged back into a heavy bun. For a moment the girl looked frantic; she hurriedly clapped the hat back on her head and pushed the thick coil of hair back out of sight.

Helen frowned. 'How peculiar!'

'Perhaps the sun does drastic things to her hair,' I suggested.

'No, I don't mean that. I must be suffering from hallucinations or something. I could swear that girl keeps following me about.'

'You couldn't mistake that dress,' I commented. 'Or that Disasterville hat.'

'No, and that makes it even odder. The last time I saw her she was wearing a dreamy outfit in brown and white tussah silk, a Dior limited edition if ever I saw one.'

'Are you sure?' Not that I doubted her observation; as far as other women's clothes were concerned, Helen's input was always wide open.

'Well . . . it doesn't make any sense. It must be a different girl. Why should anyone dress like a film-star one day, and your friendly local charlady the next? And come to that, why should anyone follow me about?'

'Ah, you're a woman of mystery. As you pointed out, I know nothing about you.'

She chuckled, dismissing the problem from her mind. 'It's going to be fun finding out, lover, I promise you that. That is, unless you intend to spend the rest of the night gawping out of that window.'

We clattered down the steps and into the stifling lobby. The caretaker was sweating cheerfully by the glass doors, waiting to lock up for the night. Beyond him I could see the driver of the ice-cream van get out of the cab and slam down the bonnet. Tired of waiting. He was short and stocky, and his white jacket, stretched tightly over his bulky shoulders, looked somehow incongruous, like a frilly

13

chiffon collar on a Dobermann. He climbed into the cab and slammed the door.

The air on the street was like the breath from a blast furnace; Helen and I stood on the pavement blinking, momentarily dazed by the heat. The girl in the green dress raised an arm and waggled her fingers at us. Helen shrugged at me, then grinned and waved back. The ice-cream van pulled slowly away from the kerb: it hadn't broken down after all.

'So you do know each other,' I said.

Helen giggled. 'But of course, my dear. That must be Jane Bond, the second deadliest secret agent in town.'

Out of the corner of my eye, I saw the van do a leisurely U-turn, and come bumbling back to us.

'The second deadliest?'

'Naturally, I am the deadliest. And to prove it, I am now going to lure you to your apartment and love you to death.'

But she never did. She was still smiling when the first bullet slammed her against the wall.

A thing had reared up in the back of the ice-cream van: a monstrous thing, like an ape with a shapeless pink blob for a head, jutting from massive, shaggy shoulders. The thing braced itself against the counter, and jabbed with a stick at one of the glass shutters; and then the stick was a black snout spouting orange-yellow flame, and the pavement was a madhouse of blood and screaming metal. The girl in the green dress watched, her face frozen in a Halloween mask of staring eyes and gaping mouth.

Somehow, I was on the ground, rolling. I knew I had to drag Helen forward, underneath the line of fire, but my fingers tore the material of her dress. I shouted her name; she made no movement at all. Blood poured from her ruined mouth, hideously staining her new dress. Her engagement dress. There was a chaos of sounds: breaking glass, screams, shouts, screeching brakes. And over all, the dry, impersonal rattle of the automatic rifle, like a stick

14

clacking along iron railings. Something pushed me sprawling over Helen's body: pain sliced through my left arm.
My mouth was full of dust; a crack in the pavement
seemed to swell into a black ravine, reeking of cordite and
blood. Sweat poured off my face into the ravine; the blackness narrowed into a long jagged crack, crawling with flies.
The firing had stopped; other noises swam into perspective.
Feet scrunched on broken glass. I pushed my weight off
Helen's body, and looked up. It was an ordinary-looking
street, dusty and sun-scorched; and people were bleeding
to death in it. A battlefield. Bullets flying, people dying.
My brain was out of control, chiming with senseless
rhymes. The rising pressure of hysteria was an excruciating,
swelling pain in my chest, and my ears were full of an intolerable, high-pitched screaming. Helen was dead. The
thought had no meaning. It flashed on and off inside my
numbed brain, as impersonal as a neon sign. The pavement lurched sickeningly, and wrinkled like a loose carpet.
Somebody tried to lift me up; I fell backwards, struggling
helplessly, like an overturned bug. Faces peered down at
me; kindly, pink faces, blurred at the edges. Among them
was the girl in the green dress, her mouth opening and
closing soundlessly, like a fish. A brown man in a grey
suit looked earnestly into my eyes. He enunciated slowly
and clearly, as if he were speaking to a foreigner: 'It's alright. You're alright. I've just phoned for an ambulance.'
Then, horribly, he started to rhyme, too. 'Lie back and rest,
we're doing our best.'

I thought that was terribly amusing. I laughed and cried
all over his shiny black shoes until I passed out.

Chapter Two

Detective-Sergeant Bullock settled his huge bulk delicately onto the metal-framed hospital chair, and rummaged in a grubby brief case. The other policeman stood quite motionless at the foot of the bed, watching me coldly. His name, Bullock had told me, was Archer. He was much younger than Bullock, dark and spare-bodied, gaunt around the eyes. His long, jutting chin was already blue-shadowed with beard, at eleven in the morning. His steady stare oppressed me; I closed my eyes and waited for the questions. I felt terrible. My head ached, my arm throbbed, and my tongue felt as if it was coated with rabbit fur.

'Well, now, what's all this about, eh?' Bullock's cheery smile was almost as unnerving as the fish-eye I was getting from Archer.

'I don't know,' I said wearily. 'Someone ran amok with a gun. I don't know who, and I don't know why.'

'Do you have any theories?

'Sure. They were insane.'

'Who were?'

'I just told you, I don't know.'

'Who would want to murder you?'

'Nobody. Anyway, it wasn't a deliberate thing. He was firing indiscriminately.'

'Hm.' Bullock's hand made a sound like sandpaper against his chin. 'He waited on that street a long time before making the attack. And the casualty pattern is quite interesting. Of the nine people injured, six had only minor cuts from flying glass and stone splinters and the like, the caretaker died of a heart attack; only you and Miss Simons were hit directly by any of the bullets. You see what I mean?'

'I see what you're getting at. But it still doesn't make any sense. I don't have enemies who would want to kill me.'

'What about Miss Simons?'

'That's even more ridiculous.'

Bullock still smiled, but his eyes were wary. 'So we have quite a mystery on our hands. Pity: I thought this one was going to be straightforward. Eh, Merv?'

The younger man didn't answer. He was still watching me, as tense and nervy as a hunting wild-cat. I glanced at him and was abruptly startled and shocked by the smouldering emotion behind his eyes. Anger radiated from him with incandescent force, yet his face was immobile as a stone. Unless he was a superb actor, he really hated me; and I had no idea why.

If Bullock was aware of the tension, he ignored it. 'I have to ask some routine questions, if you don't mind, sir?' he said. 'No particular significance in them you know. Just red tape.'

'Go ahead.'

'Name?'

'John Tallis.'

He wrote carefully in his notebook. 'Age?'

'Twenty-seven.'

'Nationality?'

'British.'

'Mm. . . . Now there, Mr Tallis, we've got another little mystery.' Bullock demonstrated the engaging way the wrinkles appeared at the corners of his eyes. 'You say you're British, but your accent is American. Or let's say, it sounds American to me.'

'My mother was American,' I said patiently. 'My father is an English professor employed at an American University.'

'Fair enough. There's an explanation for everything, I always say. How long did you serve in the US Army?'

'I stared at him. 'I didn't. I just told you, I'm a British citizen.'

'Yes, of course.' He pursed his lips and wrote some more. 'Occupation?'

I said carefully, 'I have been working for Mick Dooley, the demolition contractor.'

'Your passport says you're a writer.'

'How do you know what my passport says?'

'Because I've looked at it. We established your identity from the contents of your wallet.'

'My passport wasn't in my wallet. You searched my flat.'

'You can be sure that we had the necessary authority for it, Mr Tallis. You seem to be quite a wealthy man, incidentally: expensive apartment, English sports car. The destruction business must pay well.' His face was bland, expressionless.

'I inherited some money from my mother.'

'I see. Father still living?'

'Yes.'

'Thank you. We'll have to check it all out, of course. Just routine. Now, about the dead girl, Miss Simons. You knew her well?'

'We were going to be married.'

He sucked air through his teeth. 'I'm sorry. I didn't know that. Do you feel up to answering a few questions?'

'I suppose so.'

'Had she any enemies?'

'Not that I know.'

He sighed gustily. 'She seemed a nice respectable girl.'

'Is that a question?'

'No, it's the opinion of her associates at work and the few neighbours who knew her at all. But she doesn't seem to have had many close friends, other than yourself; and we haven't yet traced her parents. Do you have their

18

address?'

'No.'

'Ah. But they are still alive?'

'I don't know.'

'So you've never met them?'

'No.'

'How long have you known Miss Simons?'

'Nearly six months.'

'And she never mentioned her parents in all that time?'

'If she did, I don't recollect it.'

'Doesn't that strike you as odd?'

I shrugged. Helen hadn't talked about her family, because she had put thoughts of marriage out of her mind. But I couldn't explain that.

'Just another little mystery,' Bullock said. 'There'll be an explanation for it. At the moment, though, she's something of an enigma. For instance, there's that wedding ring she was carrying in her handbag. Was that hers?'

I was startled. 'I don't know. I didn't even know she had one.'

'Was she married? Or perhaps I should say, had she been married?'

The room tilted and swam gently out of focus. I closed my eyes against the dizziness and listened to my own voice saying, 'No. I'm sure she hadn't been married.'

'What makes you so sure?'

I couldn't be sure. It was difficult to concentrate. I felt as if someone was trying to unscrew the top of my head with ice-cold pincers. Bullock coughed apologetically. 'You didn't go away together—say, to an hotel. where she might feel the need of some camouflage. . . ?'

I shook my head. I wished he would stop talking about her. I could hear them moving about and muttering to each other, but I couldn't make out what they were saying. I opened my eyes reluctantly. Bullock was holding up a grey suitcase. 'Recognize this?'

It was a grey hide suitcase, not new, but not shabby,

either. 'It's pretty nondescript,' I said.

'There's a chalk-mark on this side. Does that help?'

'Yes. I have seen it before, in Helen's flat. In the hall closet.'

'Good. Now, did Miss Simons use this case a lot?'

'I've never seen her use it at all."

'Have you ever looked inside it?'

'No, of course not. It was just stowed away at the back of the closet, with the other cases. I assumed it was empty.'

Bullock balanced the case on a chair and snapped open the locks. 'Have you seen this before?' It was a black dress.

'No.'

'What about these?' He pulled out a skirt, a couple of sweaters and a few lacy handkerchiefs. I shook my head doubtfully. 'They don't ring any bells. But that doesn't prove anything. They could be old clothes she was planning to throw away.'

'Maybe. But if they are her things—and the dresses seem to be the right size—I wonder why the laundry and dry-cleaning marks are different from the rest of her clothes?'

Dizziness drifted over my mind like a fog. I began to tremble. The answer was so obvious that there had to be a catch in it somewhere. 'She changed her laundry,' I croaked. The room was suddenly like a reflection in a distorting mirror : geometrical lines disintegrated, melted into lewd, bulging shapes. Bullock's smile seemed to slide off his face and hover in the air above my head. His voice boomed hollowly, as if he was calling through a drainpipe. 'Better get the nurse, Merv. He's pretty crook.' Then to me : 'You'd better rest now, Mr Tallis. We'll see you later.'

My tongue felt clumsy and soft, like foam rubber. 'I bet you say that to all the pretty crooks,' I mumbled.

Nobody laughed, not even me. The room distintegrated some more. Bullock's smile floated away into the distance.

The gaunt detective watched me a moment longer, his dark eyes boring through the thickening grey mist. Then, abruptly, he was gone. He still hadn't said a word. But his hatchet face and lean frame stalked broodingly through my ghost-laden dreams.

If you didn't look too closely at his eyes, the surgeon looked about nineteen. He giggled a lot, as if the whole subject of bullet-wounds was a faintly indelicate joke. 'Not too much muscle-damage,' he said happily, 'but there's a slight infection, possibly from the bullet itself. Dangerous in the old days, but with these new drugs—pow!' He made a large gesture with his arm, to demonstrate the power of the new drugs. 'How do you feel?'

'I can't stop shivering.'

'That's the drugs. Depressed?'

'Suicidal.'

'That'll be the drugs too, I expect.' He sounded as if he was trying to convince himself. 'Basically, you're in good shape. You were hallucinating for a while?'

'I guess so.'

'That's the fever. And the shock, of course,' he said doubtfully. 'Touch of physiotherapy soon: repair work on those arm muscles. You're a lucky bloke. Have you bobbish as a butcher-bird in no time.'

The nurse with the flat green eyes and the chin like a sexton's spade sat on the edge of my bed and regarded me coyly. Not a pretty sight. 'You were quite delirious for a while, you know. Said some pretty fruity things, I can tell you.'

'I'm sorry if I embarrassed you, nurse,' I said.

She breathed deeply, pushing her bosom against the stiff material of her uniform. 'Call me Marje, formality's a lost art around here,' she said. 'Is it true you're an International Playboy? I never met one before.'

'No.'

'It's what the papers said. Your were all over the front page for a couple of days. Well, you meet all sorts in Casualty. Is it true you don't know who did it?'

'Quite true.'

'You can tell me, I wouldn't breathe a word. Was that really your fiancée that got shot?'

'Yes.'

'That's terrible, it really is. It's an awful feeling, to lose someone you love. I can genuinely condole, because I lost my boy-friend only a few days ago. Not killed or anything, but as good as. He went with a sister from Maternity.'

'What a shame.'

'So here's little me, footloose and fancy free again, as you might say.' She crossed one elephantine leg over the other with a sound like logs crackling in the fire. 'I oughtn't to be sitting here chatting really, but I wanted to offer my sincere condolences, because I feel I understand. We're in the same boat actually, in a way.'

She probably intended it as a kindness. 'Thank you,' I said helplessly.

'Sometimes we all need a friend to turn to. I just wanted you to know that I'm here.' Her face slowly turned a brick-red colour.

'Yes. Thank you.'

Still red-faced, she stood up and began to straighten the bedclothes with unnecessary vigour. 'The police are utterly baffled, so the papers say. Isn't it peculiar that Miss Simon's parents haven't come forward? There's been appeals on the TV and everything. And isn't it weird about all the money?'

'What money?'

'Didn't they tell you? The money they found in an old suitcase in her flat, under some clothes. Thousands of dollars, the papers said.'

Mick Dooley and a couple of the men came to see me, and stood around looking awkwardly reverential and dwarfing

22

the furniture. Mick cast a professional eye around the room, as if he was calculating what was worth salvaging. He carried a paper sack containing grapes, bananas, apples, nuts, chocolate, passion fruit and a quart of whisky. 'I brought ye a drop of the real stuff,' he whispered hoarsely, tucking the bottle under the bedclothes. 'But whatever you do, don't mix it with the Aunty Biostics. It's murder!'

The last word suddenly struck him as being unfortunate. He hurried on to cover his confusion : 'That owd theatre now, you was right about that. I should niver have touched it.'

'More demonstrations?'

'No, the bloody place is all subsidised at one end. It's a death-trap. I've got to prop it up before I can pull it down. The whole contract's worth less than a politician's handshake.'

I made conventional sympathetic noises. We were all inhibited by their best clothes and parlour manners. And there was something on their minds. After some foot-shuffling, one of them got it out : 'Have they caught the sod that done it, yet?'

'No.'

'Listen, boy,' Mick said earnestly, 'we're mates, aren't we? Give us yer hand here. Now this is it : you know you've only got to say the word, that's all. Just say the word.'

I didn't know which word to say. 'Well. . . .'

'Right yez are. Just tell us where to find that shit-eating bastard, and we'll bring yez his ballocks in a string bag. No hairy-arsed haythen is going to shoot down one of my people and live to brag about it. Leave the pollis out of it, boy; slip us the word, and I'll illuminate the savage personally.'

'I honestly don't know who it was,' I said. 'Or why it happened.'

Mick looked hurt. He thrust a bristly chin close to my face. 'Jaysus, you can trust me, boy. On me word of honour. Whatever's on your conscience is your own affair. Give me

23

that blagyard that done you, and I'll scroonge him till the pips squeak.'

'You have to believe me,' I said. 'I don't know who it was.'

The three men looked sadly at each other. I had disappointed them.

Gradually, Mick's brow cleared, and he struck the side of his head a prodigious blow with his fist. 'I unnerstand!' he shouted. 'The whole bloody place is buggered! Microphones everywhere, I'll be bound. Bluebottles taking down every blessed word! I've seen the style of it on the telly. Jeese, but they're foxy, them pollis!' He put his massive hand over my mouth, and winked so energetically that it looked as if one side of his face had collapsed. 'Of course you don't know who done it,' he bellowed. 'You'ld have told the pollis else. Naturally. We'll be off now. Let us know if ye have any errands—any little thing you'ld specially like seeing to!'

Winking, nodding, and bursting with their own subtlety, the three huge men tiptoed from the room. After they had gone, I uncapped the whisky, and took a long swig from the bottle. Mick was right. On top of the Aunty Biostics, it was murder.

The physiotherapist was a squat barrel of muscle, with the thickest forearms I'd ever seen. He called me 'cobber'—the first time I had ever heard anybody use the word—and he said 'beaut' twenty-three times in the first fifteen minutes. It was the first time I had thought of Australia as a foreign country. He barked orders, and I did the exercises without thinking or caring. He said the arm was going to be 'corker'.

Bullock and Archer came back, and took up their old positions by my bedside as solemnly as if they had been hallowed by tradition. Bullock asked the same questions and compared the answers with his notebook. Archer still didn't say a word. He stood and watched me with the same bleak malevolence, tinged with a new emotion I couldn't read. A look almost of sardonic amusement, or grim satisfaction.

24

Whatever it was, it did nothing for my peace of mind.

Bullock showed me a thick cardboard folder full of photographs. 'Do you recognize any of these men? I'm thinking particularly of the van driver. He wasn't wearing a mask, like the other fellow.'

I looked through them and shook my head.

'Does anyone there resemble our man at all?' Bullock prompted.

'They're all a bit like him.'

'Hm. But you would recognize him again?'

I shrugged non-committally. Which was unfair of me. I would know that driver again anywhere, any time.

Bullock stowed the photographs away again. 'We found twenty thousand dollars in that suitcase,' he said. 'Did you hear about that?'

'I was told. By somebody who read it in the newspapers.'

'I don't suppose you know anything about that money? Where it came from? Whose it was?'

'No.'

'You see, we've gone into Miss Simons' finances pretty thoroughly. We know what she earned, what she paid in rent, what she had in her bank account. There's no way she could have saved that money out of her income.'

'I see.'

'Did you give it to her?'

'No.'

'Ah, well. Here's another little thing that we found. What do you make of this?'

He handed over a small brown envelope. Inside was a woman's wrist-watch, gold fronted. On the stainless steel back a lovers' knot was engraved, enclosing the initials H.S. and J.S.

I said numbly, 'Where was this?'

'In the suitcase with the other things.' Bullock paused, and added gently, 'I asked you before if Miss Simons had ever been married. Let me put it another way. Can you prove that she wasn't?'

25

'No.'

'Does the name Heidi Saxon mean anything to you?'

'No.'

'Does anything strike you about the name?'

'It has the same initials as Helen Simons.'

'Exactly. The classic pattern of the alias. Well now, we have just one more thing to show you.'

It was an airmail envelope, crumpled and greasy, with yellow stains on the back. It had been posted in Japan a year earlier, and carried the trademark of a famous camera manufacturer. It was addressed to Mrs Heidi Saxon, 15a Frank Street, Woolloomooloo. There was nothing inside.

'Was this in the suitcase too?' I asked.

'No. We found that in Miss Simons' handbag, stuffed right down at the bottom under the keys and compact and the other odds and ends. You see the possibility, Mr Tallis? If Helen Simons was an alias, it explains a number of things. It explains the wedding ring, the watch, the envelope and the laundry marks. It could explain why her parents haven't been traced yet. It doesn't explain the money, or why she was killed. But there'll be a connection; there has to be.'

He watched intently, his cheerful expression at odds with the calculations behind his eyes. I was simply bewildered. My mind struggled with the implications—Helen married, leading a double life, hiding banknotes in an old suitcase. I could make no sense of it at all. And yet . . . how much do people know of each other? Against my will, my mind probed into half-forgotten corners, digging up memories of trivial, insignificant remarks and events. Every slight ambiguity, however innocent-seeming at the time, now looked strangely sinister in this new light.

Bullock gave up waiting for my comment. and changed the subject. 'Are you interested in photography, Mr Tallis?'

'Interested, but not efficient. Why?'

'There's an expensive camera and some other photographic equipment in your flat.'

'Just basic stuff.'

'I wouldn't know that. It looks pretty complicated to me. But the thing is, those stains on the envelope—the lab boys say they could have been picked up in a photographer's dark room.'

'Not in mine. I don't have a regular dark room. And I've never seen that envelope before.'

Bullock had run out of questions. He made a few perfunctory enquiries about the state of my health, and warned me to contact him, if I planned to leave the city. Archer followed him out, pausing in the doorway to look back at me. For a moment, I thought he would speak at last. But he merely nodded his head slowly, his unblinking stare giving the gesture a chilling significance. I was glad when he went away.

One detail nagged at me: there was one question Bullock hadn't asked. And that was strange, because it was the kind of coincidence policemen get curious about. A large area in Woolloomooloo was being re-developed; and I had worked with Mick's demolition company on that project. We had torn down 15a Frank Street, along with several other houses, only eight months earlier. Only a few weeks before I met Helen for the first time.

Chapter Three

The day they let me out of hospital, I went to see Gillian.

Gillian was one of the first friends I had made in Australia. She had found me a few jobs early on, writing commercial copy for a few near-bankrupt advertising companies; later on, when she learnt that I didn't really need the money, and that I had no intention of joining the long list of her lovers, she had dropped me as a thoroughly unsatisfactory prospect. She called herself a Press Agent, but in fact, she set her hand to anything that might turn a dollar. She claimed, probably truthfully, that she knew everybody in show business; and her stock-in-trade was her list of contacts.

Gillian worked on the sixth floor of a shabby block in Potts Point. Her office was reached by way of an ancient oak-panelled lift, which hiccupped from stage to stage in a series of petulant leaps, as if it were being rhythmically goosed from below. The office itself was only marginally bigger than the lift, and was as humid as a Turkish bath. It was grotesquely untidy: a chaos of paper, photographs, boxes, bottles and cigarette-ash. Gillian sat serenely in the midst of it all, crooning into the telephone, making a sales pitch. She was a fleshily handsome woman in her late forties, with a wide, sensuous mouth, and brutally-bobbed yellow hair. She was smoking, as usual.

I moved a stack of pamphlets off the clients' armchair and sat down. She finished the call with a babble of small-talk, and looked at me approvingly, tilting her head back and trickling smoke from her nostrils.

'Didn't waste any time, did you my darling?' she said. 'Wise boy.'

'What?'

'All that coverage last week. Sensational. Just the right time to cash in. I can do a lot for you, feller. As a matter of fact, you could do a lot for me, if you put your mind to it.' She fanned herself with her hand. 'Don't mind me. It's the heat. And talking to those screaming queens all day long. Stirs the hormones. Anyway, I've learned to be blunt; I wasted half a lifetime being subtle. Now, what do you want? Interviews on the telly? Sell your amazing revelations to the papers? No sweat.'

'No thanks, Gill,' I said. 'I'm buying, not selling.'

'What I have in mind right now, you could have for free.'

'Gill, I'm trying to trace a girl. Age about twenty; five-foot three or four; long platinum hair; ritzy dresser. I think she is, or was a dancer.'

'Ritzy dresser? You mean her clothes were expensive? Or just fancy?'

'Expensive, I should say.'

'In that case, she's either successful, or married to some rich bloke. Either way, she shouldn't be hard to find. What do you want her for? Or shouldn't I ask?'

'I just want to talk to her.'

'That's what they all say. Nothing illegal?'

'What's illegal about talking to a girl?'

Gillian carefully lit another cigarette from the stub of the last one, and scrabbled under a pile of letters for an ashtray. 'I don't like it,' she growled. 'I get bad vibrations. Especially when you give me evasive answers. What has this got to do with that gun-battle you were mixed up in?'

'She was a witness,' I said.

'So leave it to the fuzz.'

'I can't just sit around. I've got to do something, even if it's useless.'

She eyed me narrowly through her smoke-screen. 'Hung-up, huh? How do you think this blonde kid can help you?'

'I don't know. I'd just like to talk to her.'

'Crazy. That bullet's unhinged your mind. Why don't you get yourself another woman for a while? Therapy, sort of. I know one who'd sacrifice herself in a good cause.'

'No,' I said. 'Not yet.'

'Okay. Give me a day or two. I'll see what I can do.' Gillian scooped up a ragged bundle of newspapers from the floor, and flipped through them. 'Here you are : front page stuff for a couple of days, after that it's two inches on page four, under the margarine ads. Such is fame, buster.'

The tabloid had separate fuzzy pictures of Helen and me. She looked plumper in the face than I remembered. It seemed suddenly as if she had been dead for centuries. Gillian studied the pictures for a long moment, the cigarette dragging her mouth down in a wry grimace. 'Now where have I seen that face before?'

'With me, probably.'

'No, this is something else. . . . Was she in the business?'

'Show business? No.'

'Funny, I get show-business vibrations. Probably because you mentioned a dancer. Listen, if I find this kid, and you ask her your questions, what difference will it make?'

'None, probably.'

'That's what I thought. Look, I got a better idea. Why don't you take me out for a meal and a few drinks, and see if you can seduce me in your air-conditioned apartment?'

'Come off it, Gill,' I said. 'You could never stop smoking long enough to get laid.'

She widened her eyes in mock horror. 'Christ, do you have to stop smoking?'

I drove over to Lomond Street, off Quay West, where the theatre was. A white Holden followed me all the way, and coasted slowly past as I manoeuvred in a parking place. It was Archer, and he was alone. He crawled past, making sure that I saw him, but he didn't stop. I locked up the

Lotus, and walked down to the theatre.

The area round Quay West, one of the oldest parts of the city, has a battered charm of its own. Terraces at all angles and levels; breathtaking glimpses of blue water at the far end of narrow streets like dark, brown-walled tunnels; dusty trees casting thin shadows on the cobble-stones. The passion for redevelopment, which has made a disaster area of the city centre in recent years, was not so apparent here. The only building threatened was the theatre in Lomond Street. The scaffolding was in place, and machinery was lined up neatly under the shabby marquee, but the place seemed to be deserted. However, Mick's car was parked outside—a white sports job, one of the few in Sydney that could out-pace the Lotus—so I guessed he wouldn't be far away.

He was sitting morosely on a beer-crate in the dusty foyer. 'Can ye believe it!' he shouted. 'I'm waiting for the bloody builders! Come, and I'll show ye.'

He pressed the button that started the diesel generator for the working lights, and we went inside. The roof was off the auditorium proper, and the crew had started to strip the circle and balcony; but it was obvious that the work had been abandoned in a hurry.

'Would ye believe I daren't touch another brick until I have the wall buttressed from the other side?' Mick said. 'One swing of the hammer, and that whole section is like to topple on the supermarket next door. Will ye look at this!'

He led the way through a narrow door in the proscenium wall and down a steep flight of stairs. 'This is the cellar under the stage. Twenty feet deep. Used as a store. Packed solid with junk for years. When we shifted the junk, we found the problem.'

He pointed to a crack in the floor by the near corner. The crack was about six feet long, and four inches across at its widest point.

'Subsidence?' I asked.

'Worse than that. Listen!'

I put my ear close to the crack. There was the slightest

31

whisper of sound. 'What is it?'

'Water! There's a bloody unmapped stream under that corner. And it's hacked out a cave—God knows how big!'

I shivered involuntarily. We were standing at the base of a seventy-foot-high wall that was apparently resting on nothing.

'The Surveyor says we have to put girders in, and hydraulic jacks. Cost a fortune.'

'This place has been flooded more than once,' I said. 'You can seen the flood-marks on the walls.' The lowest of the marks was four feet above my head. I breathed a lot easier when we were safely out of there.

'Now then,' Mick said, 'you'll be after needing help to nail them murthering bastards.'

'That's right.'

'God. You don't have to tell us the details. Just the names, and where we can pick 'em up.'

'Mick, it's the honest truth: I don't know who they were.'

'Good God Almighty!' Mick was aghast. 'You mean you was done over by strangers?' His code obviously required certain formalities between murderers and their victims. 'My, that's turrible!'

'What I really need is information,' I said. 'Who really controls the action in this town?'

'Depends on the kind of action you mean. This is the age of specialization, boy.'

'I'm just grabbing at straws, Mick. I don't know where to look, or what to think. But Helen's murder had all the marks of a gang operation.'

'Gang, is it?' Mick laughed. 'Sorry, no disrespect intended, but you can be a bit naive sometimes. Your modern scallywags, see, they might co-operate on a particular caper, but they don't stick together like a footboll team.'

'What about the Syndicate and the Mafia?'

'Oh, them American things.' He dismissed them. 'Of course we have had some organizations in the past. The North Shore Mob for instance: that lasted for years until

32

the coppers finally broke it up. Protection racket: collected from all the brothels and most of the unlicenced clubs, that sort of thing. There's been nothing of that size since.'

I said: 'When an organization like that breaks up, it leaves a power vacuum behind. Who protects the brothels now?'

Mick pressed his nose flat with his thumb. 'Be damned if I know,' he said softly. 'But I know how you could find out.'

'How?'

'Ask some of the wee whores up at the Cross. Would ye believe, some of them gels would do anything for money.'

'Maybe I will.'

'Don't expect too much from it, mind. I wish there was something solid I could do to help ye.'

'There's one thing you might do. I'm looking for a man. I don't know anything about him except that he's got form.'

'I can maybe do something there. Any number of petty crooks tip their hats to me. D'ye know his name?'

'John Parvo.'

'Him!' Mick waggled his eyebrows in disbelief. 'I didn't know that knucklehead was still alive. I thought his brains had been beaten out years ago.'

'You know him?'

'I know about him. Was a boxer. Middleweight. No class. Too slow on his feet, and too slow in the head. His last fights, he was just a chopping block. Pitiful. So he's been in the nick, has he? See, there was something else I heard about him—something sorrowful—what was it now?'

'Do you think you can find him?' I interrupted.

'Surely. Why do you want him?'

'I think he was the driver of that ice-cream van.'

Mick whistled. 'But—' for a moment, he was lost for words— 'But you said you didn't know who they were?'

'I still don't. I'm not sure about Parvo; I shan't be sure until I see him in the flesh. I've only seen a picture.'

'Where?'

33

'The police showed me a whole batch of photographs.'

'And you picked out Johnny Parvo for them?'

'Not for them. For me.'

Mick's turnip-face wore an expression I'd never seen on him before. He was concerned for me. 'Are ye sure it wouldn't be best just to go away for a while and forget it? Get some sun and some rest. You look older than you should, son. And there's a mad glint to your eye.'

'I'll have plenty of time to rest, Mick. I've got nothing particular to do with my life. Apart from one thing.'

Mick grunted. 'I don't like it. I wish I'd never offered to help ye. It'll only make matters worse.'

'Helen's dead. There isn't anything worse.'

He stirred at a pile of rubble with his boot. 'If ye believe that,' he said balefully, 'then your college education was a criminal waste of money.'

Archer tailed me blatantly all the way to Woolloomooloo, but again he didn't stop or speak when I parked the car. The Lotus made his job too easy; if I wanted to lose him, I would have to use something less conspicuous.

The redevelopment programme in Frank Street had not progressed very far; the upper part of the street was just as the bulldozers had left it, a dusty, brick-strewn wasteland. The only additions were a few bright cairns of empty Coke tins and broken beer bottles.

I had no recollection at all of what had stood there. I walked down the hill. Part of the wasteland had been temporarily fenced-off as a children's playground. Perspiring Mums sprawled on the benches, exposing reddened faces and thighs to the sun, while their kids squealed and ran about on the baking asphalt. Grey dust hung in the still air.

The houses in the lower half of the street were also due for demolition soon, it seemed. Many of them were derelict and neglected. Tufts of grass grew between the paving stones. A wooden awning threw a welcome patch of shade on the pavement. A milk bar.

Behind the counter, a balding young man in an orange tee-shirt was reading the racing pages. ''Ow yer goin', mate?' he said. He folded the paper and put it back in the rack. I asked for a cold drink.

'Seen you before, an't I?' He was taking his time serving me, avid for conversation, for a bit of company.

'Probably. I worked on the demolition job, up the street.'

'Oh yerse? Filled the bloody shop with dust, that did, day after day. Never forget a face, me. Not that I see many bloody faces, these days.'

'Business bad?'

'Whaddyer think? Pullin' the whole bloody place down, an't they? Dunno when to stop, some people. Bloody shop'll be gone in a couple o' years. Nobody down here now, 'cept a handful o' grannies who got nowhere to go. Shove 'em in the work'ouse, soon as their leases is up. Fascist pigs.'

I wasn't sure whether he meant the grannies, or the people evicting them. Probably both. I said, to keep him going, 'Have you lived here long?'

'Yerse. Only got to stick it for a couple more years, though. Then it's up stakes and away. At last. At bloody last.'

'Where will you go?'

'I tell you mate, it's what I've always dreamed about. I'm goin' up North.' His little round face went pink with enthusiasm, and his eyes grew moist. 'Get me a job as a boundary-rider on the farthest station I can find. Get me out of the rat-race once and for all.'

Another city romantic, spellbound by the lure of that vast empty continent just over the horizon. No use pointing out that it was empty for the very good reason that only the toughest humans could survive in that hostile terrain; the call of the outback was very strong, particularly to those idealists who had never seen it.

I nodded at the empty, sunburnt street. 'Not the hairiest rat-race in the world,' I commented.

'Yerse, but what about when the building starts? Anyway, it's not just one street. It's the whole city. The attitudes, the injustices. Capitalist oppression, the old-boy network, vicious anti-worker propaganda, not to mention the Fascist lackeys of the State—' He stopped in mid-harangue, his brow clouded with suspicion. 'Hey! Are you another of 'em? Another bloody copper?'

'No, I told you. I work for a demolition company.'

'Oh yerse, I forgot. Bloody cops have been pestering me all week.'

I looked sympathetic. 'Police persecution?'

'Too bloody right. Endless bloody questions about some pro that lived in one of the houses up the street. Did I remember her they said. Course I bloody did, and her mate an' all, but I wouldn't give them sods the time of day.'

'You didn't tell them anything?'

'Nah. Whaddyer think? "Your bloody Gestapo methods won't work on me", I said, and they slunk off. They keep coming back, though.'

'They must think you know something useful.'

'Nah. Persecution for persecution's sake. Christ, I haven't seen either of them tarts for munce. And the bloody house where they lived has been pulled down, even. Seems the dark thin one got herself murdered or something. Well, if they're on the game, that's the risk they take, ask me. Only, they're not going to pin it on me, that's for sure.'

'Did you have to identify her?'

'Nah, but they showed me a picture. Same tart. Couldn't mistake that snooty look. Sly bitch, I always reckoned.' He poured himself a Coke and leaned his elbows on the bar, in the conventional gossip's pose. 'They weren't here all that long: probably got a cheap lease because the place was due to come down. Lived in that three-storey brick house, used to stand on the corner. Number fifteen. Divided into three flats—Dawn had the ground floor, this dark girl the middle, and some newspaper fellow the top. Never saw much of him though; he was away a lot. Funny thing, not many folk in the street knew what they were up to. I

36

twigged 'em right off. The little cuddly one used to come in here with her great big norks practically hangin' out of her blouse. Very juicy. Told me I could call her Dawn. Would you believe, I was mug enough to give 'em credit? Course, they pissed off without paying.'

'They left in a hurry, then?'

'Well, everybody had to go, see, because of the demolition order. But I thought they'd stay on till the end of their leases, like everybody else. But one morning, a big furniture vans rolls up, strips out all the furniture, and that's the last I ever see of 'em.'

'You didn't try to trace them? To get your money back?'

'Not worth it. Only a few dollars. It's the thought that hurts, though. Makes you sick when the working classes turn on each other.'

I was feeling pretty sick myself, but not on account of the working classes. I walked slowly back up the hill to my car. Beyond the playground, the street was a dusty grey desert landscape. There was not a scrap of shade here; the road surface was blistered and wrinkled by the heat, and the paving-stones were like hot coals. I remembered number 15 now: a tall, ugly house at the end of a terraced row. I remembered it quite clearly, because of the odd circumstance. When we came to pull it down, we found it still fully furnished. The shopkeeper had been quite wrong about that furniture van.

I left the car where it was, and picked my way through a zig-zag system of narrow alleys and steep steps to the western fringes of King's Cross. I walked slowly, but sweat was dripping steadily from my nose and chin by the time I reached the top, and my lungs laboured in the humid air. I saw no sign of Archer, but I assumed he wasn't far away. I hoped he was as uncomfortable as I was.

I found what I was looking for in one of the side streets by the Metro Theatre. She was pressed into the meagre shade of a doorway, keeping out of the sun and out of view

37

of the police patrolling the main street. Her sibilant whisper
flicked out at me across the pavement: 'Looking for somebody, darling?'

'Sure,' I said. 'You'll do.'

Her eyes narrowed in rapid appraisal. Her young, un-
formed face was framed by an Afro hairstyle in a dreadful
shade of pink. The heat was butchering her makeup, and
her thin dress showed dark semicircles under the armpits.
She had to be desperate, to be working in this heat.

She had her own method of assessing a client. She examined my shoes, and made a rapid calculation. 'Fifty
dollars?' She wasn't even convincing herself. Her tone was
an open invitation to haggle.

I said: It might be worth it. That depends.'

'Depends on what?' The smile stayed in place, but the
eyes were sharp, suspicious.

'On whether you can sell me what I want.'

'Oh.' Contempt showed through the relief. 'No problem,
mister. But the variations cost extra. What's your kick,
friend?'

'Talk,' I said. I slipped a few tens out of my billfold. 'I
just want you to talk to me.'

Her glance signalled the opposite pavement. 'You some
kind of nut, or something? Better be careful mister; I got
friends.'

'Sure you have. I'd like to meet some of them. I want
some information, and I'm willing to pay for it.' I showed
her the money.

'Information?' She was still wary.

And older woman crossed the road to join us. She had
an unhealthy, blue-white face, a black wig and eyes like
beads. 'Trouble, Honey?'

'This joker says he just wants to talk,' Honey said. 'I
think he's a nut.'

'Not fuzz, anyway. They're not mugs enough to work
alone.' Bead-eyes thrust her head at me. Her breath had
a graveyard stink. 'Piss off, meathead. You want to get

done for indecent exposure? Me and Honey both saw you take it out and wave it around, didn't we darling?'

'Sure we did,' Honey grinned.

'You're throwing away easy money,' I said. 'I just want to know who collects the weekly insurance? Who provides your protection?'

The women exchanged glances. The younger one appeared to be holding her breath. Bead-eyes answered for them both: 'I don't know who you are, but you're crazy, man. That's a mean scene. Talk like that could get you an extra mouth, about six inches below the one you got. Savvy? It ain't good for our health, either. Now, just sod off and leave us alone.'

'The auction could go higher,' I said. I tore out a page of my diary and scribbled my phone number on it. 'I'm prepared to better the offer if you change your mind.'

I held out the scrap of paper. Neither of them made any move to take it. I dropped it on the pavement between us. Its fluttering created an extra tension, scraping at the nerve endings. I could feel their eyes boring into my back as I walked down the hill.

I had to face my apartment eventually. Daylight was fading as I pushed open the front door against the accumulated pile of mail stacked behind it. The place smelt musty, unused; and the faint reek of stale cigarette-smoke—a reminder that strangers had pawed through my belongings—made my skin crawl.

As I picked up the mail, something clinked and slid away into a corner. It was a locker key, with a red plastic knob for a handle. It wasn't mine: I'd never seen it before. I skimmed through the letters: maybe it had slipped out of an envelope.

The phone rang and I picked it up automatically. Gillian's voice competed with rock music and shrill squeals of laughter. She was a little drunk herself. 'Johnny? Where've you been, I've been trying to reach you for ages. Listen, I've remembered where I saw that bird of yours, that Helen or whatever her dam' name was. The fact is—you're not going to like this, Johnny . . . Christ, I can hardly hear myself speak. I'm at some lousy party at Paddo, God knows why. . . . Can you hear me? Look, if you don't know this already, it's better that you get it from a friend. Your girl was no saint, Johnny.'

'I never believed she was, Gill. What are you getting at?'

'Look, darling, I'm a cynical, withered old bag who'd swap her grandmother for a cupful of sugar, but I was shocked, Johnny. No, worse than shocked. Sickened. I love you, Johnny, love you as a friend, you know? Don't spy and pry any more. Please.' She hiccuped and wheezed gustily into the phone.

'Gill—what is it? Have you traced that dancer?'

'No, and I'm not going to. I want no part of it. I can't bear to see you tear yourself apart; I won't help you to do it.' Her voice diminished alarmingly; I was afraid she was going to pass out.

'Gill! Gill—please say what you're trying to say.'

'Okay.' She paused, and went on, sounding almost sober: 'Before she met you—I hope, before she met you—Helen Simons used to pose for porno pictures. Hard porn, Johnny : crude and explicit. I've seen some of them, and believe me, they weren't just filthy. It was deeper than that. They terrified me. I've never seen anything more dreadfully— lovingly—evil.'

Chapter Four

I was standing stark naked in the middle of a strange
room. It was pitch dark, and I had lost my memory. My
throat was rigid with panic, and my head was stitched
through with white-hot wires of pain. There was noise: a
dry ratchety sound that seemed to have its source in a
nodule of agony between my eyes. Nightmare shapes stood
around me, nameless yet frighteningly familiar. A word
floated into my mind, and I grabbed at it like a drowning
man at a log. *Chair.* . . . It was a chair. It was my own chair :
a blurred outline of grey and black in moonlight. I was
in my own flat, and the phone was ringing. It was two
o'clock in the morning.

The voice spoke in a high, breathless whisper, and so fast
that I could hardly make out the words. '. . . heard you up
by the old Metro today, looking for some information,
you're the bloke, aren't you? Well, I can tell you—is that
right, you want to know who the—it's on the level I mean,
about the money and all?' Terror, or some other emotion
tugged her voice erratically up and down the stave.

'Who are you?' My brain was still foggy; I had taken
one of the sleeping pills Marje had given me as a farewell
present.

'Wait a minute. Is that on the level, about the money?
You're willing to pay for—?'

'For some names, yes.'

'Well, I know a couple of. . . . You want to know who
takes the pay-off, right? For the girls, I mean?'

'Who runs the protection racket, yes.'

'Well, I mean . . . they're rough and brutal, those bastards, I should know. That's a big risk. How much is it worth, I mean?'

'How much do you want?'

It's worth plenty. I mean, the risk . . . I'd have to get away for a while. . . . Two G's,' she concluded crisply. "Straight out, no instalments. You give me the money, and I'll give you the names.'

'It's a deal. When can I see you?'

'You got the two hundred now? In cash money?'

'No.'

'Tomorrow night then: Nine o'clock. You know Carlo's restaurant?'

'Yes.' Surely she wouldn't choose somewhere as public as that?

'Park in the street outside, as near as you can get. What sort of car is it?'

'Yellow sports car, two-seater.' I told her the registration number.

'Okay. Wait there. I'll come to you if it's safe.'

'All right. But what if either of us can't make it? Or if there's no place to park?'

'I'll contact you later, as soon as it's safe.'

'Can't I contact you?'

'No.' She rang off.

I felt chilled. I was still heavy-eyed from the drug, but I knew I couldn't sleep yet. I propped myself upright in the bed and pulled the sheet up to my chest. Through the window, I could see the moon, shiny as polished chromium, riding high over the harbour. The long expanse of black water glittered secretly, like sequins on velvet.

Mick was right. Gillian was right. I should go away and leave the whole sorry mess behind. Mick and Gillian were my friends. They could look at Helen dispassionately, and see her for what she was. I couldn't do that, not yet. Probably not ever. The memories of her voice, her perfume, the texture of her skin, the warmth of her presence, were all too close to me, too real to be denied. Surely I couldn't be so wrong about someone I knew so intimately? Yet a sly inner voice whispered to me that people are conned every day into believing what they want to believe. Love *is* blind: the old cliche is no less true for being hackneyed.

I shrugged off that debate. There was only one course I could take, and no amount of sweet reason was going to divert me from it. If it turned out to be a disaster course, I couldn't say I hadn't been warned.

I thought about the key. There had been no explanation of it in the rest of my mail: no letter, no empty envelope, no tag or label. Someone had simply pushed it through the letter-box. Why? Assuming it had any significance at all—that it wasn't just a mistake or a practical joke—it looked as if someone was trying to tell me something. Or maybe it was a trap? But a trap should surely be more direct, less haphazard. Suppose I just handed the key over to the police? I might do that yet; but not before I had looked in that locker myself.

It was getting lighter. The moon faded thinly into a mother-of-pearl sky. Traffic began to move on the harbour, exhausts popping. I felt insubstantial, unreal, part of a ghost world. My thoughts rustled and whispered inside my skull like bleached old bones, paper-thin. The sleeping-pill was catching up on me. I didn't try to fight it: I needed the sleep.

The early-morning haze, shimmering over the far shore of the harbour, burned off fast. It was going to be another blistering day. I pushed the Lotus into the slow-moving stream of ingoing traffic, and queued patiently to cross the Harbour Bridge, with the sharp tang of exhaust fumes stinging my nostrils. Sunlight bounced blindingly off the white peaks of the Opera House, showing through the massive steel framework of the Bridge. Nobody followed me that I could see, but in that mass of traffic it was impossible to be sure. I made a brief call at my bank, and then went in search of the locker.

Since it was in the obvious place, at Central Station, I found it at the first attempt. I don't know what I expected to find inside, but I had assumed it was connected with Helen's murder. If it was a clue, it was certainly too big to be overlooked; but I could make nothing of it. Inside the locker were a 32-mm movie camera and a big steel box full of sound-recording equipment. They had to mean something. I lugged them out to the car and took them back to the flat.

The lift seemed to be stuck on one of the upper floors, so I carried the heavy load up the single flight to my front door. Archer caught up with me as I got the door open, and followed me into the hall. He heeled the door shut and walked round me as I stooped to put the camera and the box on the floor. When my head was at a convenient height, he punched me viciously in the jaw. My head clicked sideways and my feet tangled in the box. I was sprawled on the floor before I knew what was happening. I came up fast, but stopped short when I saw the gun in his fist. It was a short-barrelled Colt revolver; and to judge by the look in his eyes, he was crazy enough to use it.

'That's just a down-payment, you stinking ratbag.' It was the first time I had heard his voice. It came out hoarse and tight, and rasped like sandpaper. 'You'll get the rest, don't worry.'

I was raging, but as much at myself as at him. I had seen that it might be a trap, but I had walked into it anyway. Now I was neatly framed, with several thousand dollars' worth of stolen property on my hands. And Archer obviously intended to work me over before taking me in. He moved closer and swung the gun in a savage little arc, nailing the bruise on my left arm with pin-point accuracy. 'You know what I want, you bloodsucking pig,' he grated. 'Now you're going to tell me where they are.'

He was wrong on both counts, but I didn't think he would

44

believe me when I told him so. I told him anyway. He didn't believe me. He didn't even seem to be listening. He said, 'I know they're not in this place, I've stripped it clean. So you've got them hidden away somewhere.' He jabbed the gun forward, rapping the muzzle on my breastbone.

'Put that away. You're not going to use it.' I hoped I sounded calmer than I felt.

'Don't bank on it, scab.'

'You've told me too much. You think I have something you want. If that's true—and it isn't—you can't afford to kill me.'

I thought for a moment that I had gone too far : there's a limit on what you can bluff on a blind hand. But the mad glare receded a little and gave way to a look of wary calculation. He stepped away, the gun dangling from his finger. 'I should have guessed she'd pick one like you,' he muttered. 'Covered all the angles, haven't you? All except one. Now, I know who you are, Tallis. And that's a big difference, believe me. Now, we can start to even up the score.'

My jaw was beginning to ache, and the numbness in my arm was wearing off. 'I wish you'd start to think straight,' I said. 'Just accept the possibility that you've made a mistake. That I don't have what you want. That I don't even know what it is.'

'Oh, sure.' He sounded relaxed all of a sudden; even amused. 'I sussed you from the start, even before I saw you, from the eye-witness account—how you shielded yourself behind the woman's body, when she fell—'

'What!'

'You're a fast mover, Tallis. You'd have to be, in your trade. And when I did see you, you were just the kind of fat cat I thought you'ld be—fancy car, lush apartment, the whole bit. All paid for by mugs like me. And now I cop you with this—' he tapped the camera with his foot. 'Can't wait to get back in business, can you?'

It was beginning to make sense at last. 'Blackmail!' I

said. 'Someone was blackmailing you.'

'Not someone. You.'

'You're wrong.'

'Don't try to snow me, Tallis. I've got you in my sights. You think it's a stand-off, don't you? You think I daren't move, because of Mary, and because I'm a cop. But you stopped pulling the strings the moment you were flushed out into the open. Now, you and I are sitting on the same bomb, understand? You pull out the pin, you blow us both up. Because if Mary—if anybody—sees those. . . .' His jaw began to shake, and the gun came up threateningly, levelled at my stomach. 'I ought to stamp on you like a bug. When I think . . . I suppose five thousand dollars is just mouse shit to a fat pig like you, eh Tallis? Not to me, though. I sweated blood for that money, and I want it back. All of it.' He was trying to goad himself into pulling the trigger, but he wanted some reaction from me to give him the final excuse. I stood still and silent, not looking at his eyes, trying not to look at the gun. Gradually he got himself under control. 'Understand this,' he rasped. 'You're boxed-in from now on. Every move you make will be watched, every contact noted. Sooner or later you'll make a mistake, or somebody will shop you. And the moment you lose your leverage, you're a squashed bug.' He gestured with the gun. 'Open the box.'

The recording equipment was pretty sophisticated stuff. Besides the battery-operated tape-recorder and the synchro link for the camera, there were half a dozen miniature radio mikes and a UHF receiver. At Archer's instruction, I tipped everything out of the box, but he made no move to inspect it closely. 'You wouldn't be fool enough to bring them here,' he shrugged. He moved to the door and holstered the gun under his coat. 'I'll get them back someday. Soon. And when I do, if you're still around, I'll destroy you, someway or other. Only before that, I want the money back. Five thousand dollars. Have the money for my by tomorrow night.'

Everybody was after my money, it seemed. I found my voice: 'What did—how was Helen Simons involved in blackmailing you?' But I had a sickening feeling I knew the answer.

'Never give up, do you?' He grinned without humour. 'You're a trier, I'll give you that.'

'Then I'll try this,' I said. 'Did you kill her?'

The grin faded. 'I wish I had,' he said bitterly. 'But you know dam' well I didn't. And you know why.' He went away without waiting to be contradicted again.

I felt limp and exhausted. My brain was too tired to hack away at the problems any longer; and I shrank away from examining the pattern that was emerging. I took my shoes off and lay on the bed. The air-conditioner purred quietly, masking the sounds from outside. I had an appointment at nine that evening; nothing to do before then. Plenty of time to rest.

It was dusk when I woke up: the few minutes of red-tinted twilight before the sun abruptly disappeared. The rest had done me good. My jaw still throbbed, and my shoulder was sore, but the bone-weariness had left my body, and my head felt functional again. On the other hand, my clothes were a mess. I switched on the light, and started to peel off my shirt. Something smashed through the window, scattering glass, jolting my nerves like an electric shock. The thing clunked heavily on the floor and rolled in a lazy curve to the skirting-board. I recognized it at the instant of its landing, its image panic-frozen on my retina. It was a bomb.

Chapter Five

It was a Mills' hand-grenade, one of the World-War II pineapples. I dived for the far side of the bed, and pulled the mattress on top of me. It wasn't much in the way of shelter, but I was in no condition to be choosey. Even as I moved, my mind registered an oddity: the bomb should have exploded already. Three-second fuse. The seven-second fuse was decades out of date. I began to inch towards the door, pressing myself flat and dragging the mattress with me. I counted off the seconds, inwardly flinching against the explosion I expected at every stroke.

It never came.

I crawled to the door, wrenched it open, and threw myself out of the room with a convulsive leap that carried me through the hall and into the kitchen beyond. It took me two minutes of gasping for breath to register that the phone was ringing.

The voice was flat, unemotional, slightly prissy, the consonants heavily stressed. 'Relax, friend. It's a dummy.'

'What? Who is this?'

'The bomb, pal. It's a dummy. But it needn't have been, see? The next one won't be. We can pick you off any time we want to. Got the picture?'

I was still trembling. 'Who are you?' I croaked again.

He ignored the question. 'There's maybe one way you can save your skin, Johnny-boy. Put the film and the fifty thou in a suitcase, and bring the suitcase down to me, on the boat.'

'There had to be a third one,' I said. 'Everybody's after my money today.'

'What did you expect, after all that publicity? That's the last thing you need, in your racket. Get here at seven tomorrow night. On the dot. That'll give you enough time to get the stuff together. After that, if we have to, we'll come for you. It's too easy, now we know where you are, sonny. And who you are.'

'I don't suppose you're going to tell me the name of your boat? Or where I can find it?'

'Why play it stupid? We got a couple of guys here, would really enjoy digging it out of you the hard way.' He rang off before I could ask any more questions he could ignore.

The nearest I could get to Carlo's was two hundred yards down the road. I slotted the Lotus between a fat Mercedes and a beat-up station wagon, and settled down to wait. I was a few minutes late; I hoped she hadn't lost her nerve, whoever she was.

Apparently she hadn't. Heels clip-clopped along the empty pavement. A head appeared at the window. Shoulder-length hair, lank and uncombed; an overpowering stench of cheap perfume. 'Hello darlin'! Looking for—' She leaned closer, and in a staccato whisper : 'Not safe now. Carlo's—after midnight. Don't be followed.' She stepped back and made a rude noise with her lips. 'Please yourself, poofter!' she shrilled. 'Who needs you?' The heels clip-clopped a little faster, going away.

A light-coloured Falcon saloon cruised past, keeping the girl in view. My heart suddenly began to hammer at my rib-cage as if it would beat its way out. My hand shook as I reached for the ignition key.

The girl had disappeared from the main road into some side alley or doorway. I didn't see her go. The Falcon hesitated, picked up speed. I followed. I had to wait until we were stopped by traffic lights before I had a chance to see the driver's face properly. I pulled up alongside him, in the outer lane, and lowered the passenger window. 'Parvo?' I called softly.

His head swivelled like a puppet's, and his hot little eyes snapped at me. I was right. I would know him anywhere. He was my Dobermann in the frilly collar: the driver of that deadly ice-cream van.

He took off like a rocket, crashing through the gears and flogging the engine into whining protest. I followed him by pure instinct, swerving insanely through the cross-traffic in a welter of blaring horns and screaming rubber. I was grimly determined not to lose him, unless I ran out of gas before he did.

He gained a lot of ground in the first minutes by suicidal tactics, overtaking in the face of oncoming traffic, and cutting sharply across the inside lanes, forcing other cars to brake sharply; but in both speed and manoeuvrability I had too much in hand to be shaken off. As soon as I got close enough behind him again, I leaned on the horn, to attract attention. Where the hell was Archer? The suspicious bastard was supposed to be tailing me everywhere. Now I really needed him, and he was nowhere around.

I stopped sounding the horn. It was achieving nothing, other than to clear people out of our way. We swept onto the Cahill Expressway and round the tight curve that brought us up to the Harbour Bridge gates. He drove decorously here, mindful of the police patrols. I could do nothing but stick close behind him in the nearside lane. No police patrol came anywhere near us.

He began to drive faster; not recklessly, but to some purpose. He left the motorway and doubled back and forth along curving, switchback streets as vertiginous as a roller-coaster. I had no idea where I was; the suburban streets looked very like each other, and the twists and turns had confused my sense of direction. There were a few brightly-lit intersections, but we passed through them too fast to read the street-signs. We rumbled over a narrow bridge, and raced through prosperous-looking roads where the houses were set far back behind jungly gardens.

The houses thinned out, gave way to thick bush, crowding the verges of the narrow road. There were no other cars in sight; I wondered briefly if he would stop and force some kind of show-down here. But he pressed on at his own speed, making no attempt now to shake me off. I glanced at the dashboard clock. I had been chasing him for nearly an hour.

Without warning, he whipped the car into a right turn, and shot into a narrow track through the bush. I followed him easily; at that speed, I had fewer problems in tight cornering than he had. It was a better road than it looked at first sight: a thin, metalled strip, with dirt shoulder at each side. After a few preliminary wriggles, it straightened out and stretched far beyond the range of our headlights, seemingly into empty space. The bush on the left was unguarded; on the right, a tall wire fence shielded mile after mile of undulating, scrubby parkland.

The thick bush and the fence ended together; the road curved sharply uphill through jutting outcrops of rock crowned with thorn and wind-tortured ti-trees. He charged the hill as if he was trying to jump it, hit the curve at eighty, and screamed through it on the wrong side of the road, still accelerating. I stayed close on his tail, matching his every manoeuvre by force of habit now, determined not to be shaken loose. I suppose he had been counting on that.

A massive, wrought iron gate blocked the way dead in front of us.

There was no chance that he could stop short of it. He didn't even try. He swerved off the road to the right, his braking lights glaring and snaking crazily from side to side. The tail of his car seemed to be swinging uncontrollably; he side-swiped a wooden fence and skidded through it in a four-wheel drift. I had no time to do anything but follow him, if I didn't want to crash head-on into that mass of wrought iron. I jammed on the brakes, fought the car's

51

head round, and accelerated out of the skid. I shot through the gap in the fence like a bullet.

And nearly straight into space.

A gravel drive led from the wrought iron gate in a perfect circle round the perimeter of a small park on the top of a narrow headland. The central area was grassed over, and the edge of the cliff was guarded by a double line of chains strung from steel posts. The other driver had managed to stop his car by skidding into a thick clump of bushes by the gate; even so, he was only inches from the boundary fence. If I ran into him, we would probably both go over. I hit the brake hard, and hurriedly released it again : the loose gravel was as treacherous as wet ice. The fence leaped towards me; I yanked the wheel round, and the horizontal lines of chain slid past my windscreen in a nightmare motion, as if the car was going sideways. The chain was much too close, and I was going suicidally too fast, spinning round in that confined space like a deranged fly in a bottle. I managed to haul the bonnet round; the rear nearside wing struck one of the metal uprights with a jarring clang, and the Lotus, wincing reproachfully, side-stepped neatly to the right. Somehow, I jammed the gear lever into second; the engine roared and began to brake the car like a sheet anchor. She clawed her way off the loose gravel and onto the central lawn. The tyres gripped on the thick mat of buffalo-grass, and the spinning world steadied a little, as the car came under control. Relief flowed through me like a blood transfusion. Miraculously, I was alive. Thank God for modern technology, I thought. A lesser car would have been a battered tin coffin by now.

Relief was both misplaced and short-lived at that point. The Falcon had reversed out of the shrubbery, and now swung savagely in my direction. It glowed with a single eye; one of its headlamps had been smashed. His intention was immediately obvious: he had missed with the first barrel, so now he was lining up the second. He was going to use the heavier weight of his car to push mine off the cliff.

I was slewed across the grass almost at right angles to his line of attack : since hurtling through the gap in the fence, I had spun through more than a full circle. My front wheels were back on the gravel drive; whichever way I turned, I had to go dangerously near the edge, and offer him the opportunity of a flank attack. To stay tamely where I was, simply put my head on the block. Praying that I had made the right decision, I banged the car into reverse, and pulled hard round to face him. He countered by wheeling slowly to my left; so long as he could keep me trapped against the cliff edge, he held the advantage in this insane duel. Every yard I covered gave me less room to manoeuvre. I kept reversing in a tight arc, which meant going too close to the fence, but I thought if I could lure him a bit closer to the central area, I might, by changing direction unexpectedly, squeeze past him on the outer perimeter. It wasn't much of a plan; it depended heavily on my car's leaping acceleration, and it demanded split-second timing.

I waited for the right split second, stood on the brake, whipped into first gear, and stamped on the accelerator.

And stalled.

Not even the miracles of modern technology could save me from this piece of panic-stricken clumsiness. I was helpless : stuck on the edge of a God-forsaken cliff at the mercy of a homicidal maniac wielding a ton of metal as a bludgeon. A literal push-over.

He was quick to see his advantage. He moved in behind me in a wide semi-circle, coming in efficiently, without undue haste. In a panic I turned the starter key, and the Lotus lurched forward; I had forgotten that I was in gear. The car bucked like a frisky horse under an inept rider, and my feet scrabbled on the controls. Incredibly, I was aware of motion. The little car was wagging its tail like a duck. Somehow, the engine had caught, and I was trying to push the throttle through the floor. The revs whined like banshees, and the rear wheels fought for purchase on the loose gravel. My brain refused to function; I was being brutal and stupid with the machine, which was a poor return for its saving my life only a minute ago.

It saved my life again. For several seconds I couldn't figure out how the Falcon managed to miss me. It swerved away at the last second, showering the bodywork of the Lotus with a machine-gun hail of gravel. The driver was leaning forward, hitting at something with his fist: his windscreen. He couldn't see! The gravel thrown up by my rear wheels must have shattered his windscreen—the safety-glass frosting over at the moment of impact. He had pulled away from a collision course in a reflex action of self-preservation.

Before I had time to register this consciously, the Lotus leapt forward, as if in pursuit of the other car. He was trying to brake when my bonnet caught the right-hand side of his rear fender, and clawed the tail of his car round. The Falcon hit the fence head-on, snapping the lower length of chain immediately. The upper length held, but the weight of the car bent the metal posts outwards, and for an instant the whole thing was suspended grotesquely in space, like a monstrous bird entangled in a wire noose; and then it buckled and slid over the edge with a thin, teeth-grating screech of metal.

I stopped the Lotus, switched off the engine and lights, and sat with my eyes closed until I stopped shaking. It took a long time. I expected the police to arrive at any second, but they didn't. Nobody came.

I got stiffly out of the car. The breeze was chilly, and the sea noises seemed very loud. I breathed deeply, luxuriantly; I felt light-headed, as if I had been drinking on an empty stomach. My knees began to buckle, and I held on to the car door for support.

The wind rustled the dry leaves on the bushes, and the surf boomed under the cliff. There were no other sounds. No car, no sirens, no alarm bells. Nothing.

The impetus that had got me out of the car faltered to

a dead stop. I sat on the grass and stared at the invisible horizon, while the moon rose higher behind me. A passenger liner went past, glittering from stem to stern, and trailing shreds of Victor Sylvester from its tannoi system. Smaller ships passed. I watched apathetically. After a time, I went to the gap in the chain fence, and looked over the edge.

It was not as high as I had imagined. The base of the cliff was in darkness, but I could make out the ragged-lace foam of breaking surf less than a hundred feet below, and hear the sandpaper scrape of pebbles as the waves retreated. I got the torch from the car and shone it down, but its beam was baffled by the surf haze. I could make out no sign of the Falcon.

About fifty yards beyond the limit of the chain fence, where the formal park petered out into thick scrub, I found a way down. The path had obviously been pioneered by the neighbourhood kids. It was a slanting ledge about a foot wide, with a well-defined track of toe-holds, like a primitive ladder. In daylight, the descent would have been easy; in darkness, every fumble, every change of texture underfoot, made my nerves scream like a frightened hare.

Near the bottom, the rock was slimy and cold. My back was chilled too, where the wind pressed my clammy shirt against my skin; and the exertion provoked a sullen, resentful ache in my shoulder.

The ledge ended in a chaos of huge weed-covered boulders. It was tough, slippery going, and the spray drenched my clothes within minutes; but I found the car quite quickly. It was upside-down, its nose and one front wheel sticking up out of the waves at a lopsided angle. I scrambled out along the rocks as close as I dared, but the Falcon was well out of reach. It was still shifting, being pushed sideways by the shuddering impact of the big rollers. The water poured between the rocks, slapping against my thighs, then ebbed with a vicious hissing sound. Even at that depth, the tide tugged like a wild animal on a leash. I couldn't get closer without a line; the rip-tide along those rocks would tear me to pieces. And even if I could reach the Falcon, I couldn't achieve anything. He had to be dead. He wasn't going to tell me what I wanted to know.

The moon appeared over the edge of the cliff, and its pale glare lit up the narrow strip of shoreline. The rocks were black shadows edged with silver, and the plumes of spray sparkled with cold fire. The inescapable, relentless roar of the surf began to oppress me, to numb my battered senses. Tiredly, I began to stumble back the way I had come.

Then I found him.

The moonlight was reflected in a glimmer of white where no white should have been. It was his shirt. He was lying face-down in three feet of water, his right foot wedged in a V-shaped gap between two rocks. He was quite dead.

His name, according to his driver's licence, was John Ashleaf. It didn't mean anything to me. He also had fifty dollars in a cheap plastic wallet, some small change, and an assortment of keys on a ring. Nothing there to tell me why he had helped to kill Helen and tried to kill me. I shoved everything back into his pockets, and felt his wrist for a pulse. It was a waste of time, as I knew it would be: there was no flicker of life. I rolled him back into the water. Goodbye, Johnny.

It wasn't until I was half-way up the cliff face that I got the shakes again; and then I had to concentrate all my will-power on the effort of hanging on. The temptation to let go was very strong. I pressed my face against the sharp ridges of the rock until the fit passed, and then I hauled my protesting limbs up to the top.

When I got back to the car, I was walking like an old man. The effort of easing myself into the driving-seat brought tears to my eyes. Eventually, I found a main road that was signposted back to Sydney.

I ought to have phoned the police when I got in, but I didn't. I took a shower and changed into some clean clothes. It was after midnight, and I had a date waiting at Carlo's restaurant.

Chapter Six

He was short, plump and middle-aged; and his face was covered in blood. He appeared at the top of the steps, about twelve feet above me, with gaping mouth and arms outflung like a pop singer demanding applause. Two men stood behind him in the shadows, chorus figures in the drama, one bulky, the other slim. The plump man buckled at the knees and fell limply, making no attempt to protect himself, rolling and bumping down like a sack of potatoes, finally sprawling at my feet, on the first terrace. He sighed deeply and lay still. The traffic noise, already distant, seemed to recede further. The two men at the top of the steps drifted further back into the shadows, disappeared.

I knelt by the fallen man. He opened his eyes, made a gagging sound, and punched me in the face. It was a feeble effort, but it was too much for his strength. He fell back exhausted. Blood trickled from his nose and mouth.

'I'll get a doctor,' I said. 'Just stay there.' Stupid thing to say. He wasn't going anywhere.

'The girl!' he moaned, choking over the words. 'See . . . the girl. . . .'

'Lie still. I'll get a doctor.'

I raced up the remaining steps, trying to remember where the nearest phone-box was. I could phone from Carlo's, if necessary; it wasn't far away. Or perhaps there would be someone on the street who could help.

There was someone on the street, but she was not going to be any help. She was lying face downward in the gutter,

57

just beyond the pool of light from the streetlamp.

She looked dead. I turned her over gently : she was as stiff as a waxwork dummy. She wasn't dead, but rigid from shock, her eyes wide and staring, her lips drawn back from tightly-clenched teeth. It was the second time I had seen her that night. The hair was still a mess, and the cheap perfume mingled nauseatingly with the stink of blood and sweat. Now I could see her properly, I guessed she was about nineteen. The front of her cotton dress had been ripped apart, and the tattered edges were dark with blood. She trembled as I touched her, and her skin felt deathly cold. I propped her up, wrapped my jacket round her, and made comforting noises. If she heard me, she made no response.

There was not a soul to be seen. A car started up, about a hundred yards away. Its tail lights showed briefly, then it turned into a side street.

Lights showed in the front room of a house opposite. I ran over and hammered on the door. There were weird noises inside : an electronic twangling and bellowing, as of a cow with colic. I added to the din by leaning on the doorbell while I continued hammering. The door was wrenched open by an emaciated man wearing nothing but a ragged pair of denim shorts. He had shoulder-length hair and carried a guitar.

'What's the beef, Dad?' he demanded petulantly. He looked about ten years older than I, but maybe a musical career confers the privileges of perpetual youth.

I said, 'There's been an accident. Two people injured. Can you phone for an ambulance and the police?'

'Retain the cool, Pop,' he said airily. 'Haste makes waste.'

'Hurry—' I said, but he had already gone. I heard him start to dial, and then I hurried back to the two casualties.

The girl was unconscious now. The fat man was on his knees, trying to pull himself upright by the handrail. I ran down the steps and tried to support him. 'Can you make it to the top?' I asked. 'The girl's passed out, but the

58

ambulance is on it's way. And the police.'

The man sat down on the steps. 'No police,' he mumbled. 'Don't want the police. Wife—'

'Is that your wife, up there?'

'Christ, no! Thassa pro. Good kid, know what I mean? Not licenced, they said, not in the Union, they said. Used a cut throat razor to. . . . Laughed, like it was a big joke. I went for 'em. Bloody fool. Old woman'll kill me, fighting over a bloody pro at my age!'

'What did they mean, not in the union?'

'Not protected, Dumbo. Not paying her weekly dues. She was practically amateur, anyway. Cheap. Used Carlo's, see? No overheads.' The sirens brayed in the distance. 'Christ, the coppers! I got to . . . got to get away!' He lurched to his feet, panic giving him strength.

'Don't be a fool,' I said. 'You need a doctor.'

He shuffled on the edge of the next flight of steps, swaying dangerously. I grabbed for his arm, but he struck my my hand away. 'Let go of me!' I caught hold of his coat collar. His feet slipped over the edge; he fell awkwardly, trying to twist away from me. The jacket pulled down over his shoulders, pinning his arms to his sides. His wallet and some papers fell out of an inside pocket. The sirens were much closer now. The fat man began to swear in a hopeless monotone. He tore off his coat, picked up his wallet, and began to scrabble desperately for the bits of paper. They were photographs, postcard-size. I picked one up and glanced at it.

My world took a monstrous, shuddering heave into insanity.

Gillian hadn't over-stated a thing. The photograph was not just pornographic, it was sick and evil. I didn't recognize either of the men, but it was Helen's face, rapt and smiling, eyes closed in an ecstacy that looked almost religious in its fervour.

The fat man snatched the photograph from my hand, and blundered headlong down the steps, holding the hand-

59

rail. I didn't attempt to stop him this time. The pain in my chest was beyond the reach of any known anaesthetic. I wanted to be sick, but was afraid the first thing I would throw up would be my heart.

'Hey, Dad!' Long-Hair appeared at the top of the steps. 'Here come de fuzz, man. Rise up and greet the law.' He was still wearing nothing but his denim shorts, and he carried his guitar over his shoulder, like a club.

The arrival of the police had turned the scene from the sordid to the dramatic. Their car was sprawled at an angle to the kerb, and its flashing domed light gave an impression of swift, decisive action. In fact, little was going on. One uniformed policeman knelt by the body of the girl, while another propped himself languidly against the boot of the car. About half-a-dozen people watched them in respectful silence from the fringes of the pool of light.

'She's still breathing, Jimbo,' said the kneeling policeman. 'Been stabbed, looks like.'

'She'll live,' the one called Jimbo said. He sounded bored. 'Can't do anything till the doc gets here. Where's the bloke that phoned in?'

'Right here, Colonel,' Long-Hair saluted smartly. 'But Big Daddy yonder told me to.'

'Okay,' said Jimbo laconically. 'The buzz said two casualties. You the other one?' He looked in my direction and raised a languid eyebrow.

'No. The other one ran away.'

'Why?'

'He didn't want to be questioned by the police. Something about his wife.'

Jimbo glanced at the girl. 'That figures. Was this runaway, henpecked fellow also injured?'

'He looked as if he had been beaten up. And he had fallen down the steps.'

'Beaten up? Was anyone else around, when you arrived?'

'Two men, up here on the road. I was half-way down the steps; I didn't get to see them properly. One was thick-set, average height, about two hundred pounds, I guess. The other was taller and much thinner.'

He nodded, apparently without interest. 'Check the steps, Fred,' he said to the other policeman. He ambled round to the far side of the car, and reached in at the window for radio telephone. He chatted into it for several minutes in a lazy drawl.

The ambulance arrived before he had finished. The doctor made a brief examination, and nodded to the stretcher men, who began to swathe the girl in blankets. The doctor picked up my jacket and came towards us.

'Whose coat?' Careworn eyes belied a brisk and military manner.

'Thanks,' I said. The jacket was a write-off: a mess of blood and oil.

Jimbo asked : 'Carve-up?'

'Mutilation, probably with a razor or sharp knife,' the doctor said. 'Not the first one of its kind we've seen. Usual problem, I suppose?'

'Looks like it. Bloody amateur. Ought to know better, in this area.'

'Poor kid.'

'Stupid tart,' Jimbo said carelessly. 'Let me know what you find out. And how soon I can talk to her. Not that it'll make any difference. She won't tell us anything. The next thing they cut could be her throat. And she knows it.'

'The call said two casualties,' the doctor said, turning his sad eyes on me. 'You the other one?'

'No.'

'You look a bit shaky. And there's blood on your shirt.'

'I'm okay.'

Jimbo yawned. 'The other one ran away.'

'That's okay then. I don't bother with them, if they can run.' The doctor turned and marched smartly back to the ambulance. 'Merry Christmas,' he said, without turning round.

Fred returned, pink and panting. 'There's blood on the

61

first terrace,' he reported, 'and a few scattered drops on the lower steps. I went all the way down. Nobody about. There's three ways he could have gone from there.'

'Yeah, well there's not much more we can do here,' Jimbo said. 'See if you can get some help, and check the gutter and these front gardens for a weapon—knife or razor, something like that. It isn't likely, but we'd better look.'

'Jeese, I hope we can nail these bastards right soon,' Fred muttered darkly. 'They're making monkeys out of us.'

'Cool off, sonny. Relax the righteous-anger muscle. Ten to one there's been no crime committed here tonight.'

'What!'

'Unless there are witnesses—and there won't be— that kid's got to lay charges before we can say officially, that there's been any crime. And you can bet your last dollar she'll keep her little mouth shut. If she decides to tell us that she tripped and cut herself on a flying saucer, there's nothing we can do about it.' Jimbo turned to Long-Hair, who was tentatively fingering a chord on his guitar. 'Which is your house?'

'Over there, Colonel.'

'There must have been some noise when all this was going on. Didn't you hear anything?'

Long-Hair looked offended. 'Man, I was *practising*!' he said. He made it sound like an exalted mystical experience.

'In that case just give me your name and address. And if you refer to me again as Colonel, or even pig or fuzz, or any of those fashionable titles—' Jimbo's drawl became more pronounced—'I may be forced to ram your banjo up your jacksie. Thick end first.'

Long-Hair stepped back hastily. 'Promises, promises!' he muttered. But he gave the information meekly enough, and padded back across the road. He paused on the steps. 'Banjo!' he shrilled. 'Flannel-eared Philistine!' He slammed the door with a wood-splintering crash.

Jimbo turned to me. 'Would you care to come down to the station, Mr Tallis?' His manner was elaborately casual.

62

'A detailed statement would be an enormous help.'

'How did you know my name?'

'Your picture was in the papers. You were shot at by some well-organized villain. I'm always interested in famous people.'

The station wasn't far away. Fred drove us there and then went off to organize the search. Inside, Jimbo murmured something to the desk-sergeant, and then led the way up a shabby flight of stairs to a corridor lined on both sides with cell-like offices. Jimbo chose one, apparently at random, sat down behind a bare, functional desk, and pointed me to a chair opposite. He tugged open a drawer and produced a microphone. 'Tape-recorder,' he said. 'Saves a lot of time. If the bloody thing works.'

A tousled young man came in, gave Jimbo a few pages of hand-written notes, then sat unobtrusively in a corner behind me and doodled in his notebook.

The tape-recorder was not a conspicious success as a time-saver. Jimbo fiddled with it interminably before it would operate to his satisfaction; and then he took me laboriously through my account of the incident, checking and re-checking each detail with maddening deliberation. A couple of details seemed to take him by surprise. 'Wait a minute.' he said. 'You mean the fat man actually mentioned a protection racket?'

'That's what I understood him to mean. He said the girl wasn't paying her weekly dues, that she wasn't protected.'

Jimbo shook his head, as if to clear it. He took some time to frame his next question. 'What exactly was your business in that area at that time?'

'I was on my way to a restaurant.'

'Which one?'

'Carlo's.'

I had surprised him again. He let several seconds go by in silence while he studied my face. 'Why?'

I side-stepped that one. 'To eat. They stay open until 2.30.'

This time, Jimbo paused even longer. He seemed at a loss for words. Footsteps sounded heavily in the corridor, and Bullock came in. He looked hot and tired. Jimbo switched off the machine and put the microphone away. It occurred to me that he had merely been filling in time, in order to keep me there.

'I got your call,' Bullock said. 'Thanks.'

Jimbo nodded. 'Merv with you?'

'No. He's flying solo somewhere. He should be back any time.' Bullock's tone was strangely unconvincing. Jimbo glanced sharply at him, but made no comment. Bullock picked up the notes, and skimmed through them in a frowning silence. The jolly-farmer image was slipping, showing signs of the pure granite underneath. He tossed the notes aside, and jabbed a stubby forefinger at me. 'Empty your pockets.'

'Why?'

He shrugged. 'I just want to test your co-operation.'

I emptied my pockets. He arranged the contents in a neat line on the desk. 'How well did you know Miss Jones?'

'Who?'

'The girl who was attacked tonight.'

'I didn't even know her name.'

He picked up my diary. 'Your phone number—written on a page torn out of this diary–was found in her handbag.'

'I didn't give it to her,' I said truthfully.

'So you've no idea why she had it?'

'No.'

'You're lying, Tallis. D'you think we haven't cottoned on to your game?'

I didn't attempt to answer; I wasn't sure what he was talking about. Jimbo yawned and clasped his hands behind his head. 'One thing I can't figure,' he said 'is this dancer tag. You're a pretty big fellow for that kind of label.'

'Yeah, but he's light on his feet,' Bullock growled. 'A quick mover. That's why he's alive today.' He scooped up my belongings, and handed them back to me. 'Okay,' he said, 'Let's all go see if they've put the fire out.'

It sounded like a cue. 'What fire?' I asked, obligingly.

Bullock and Jimbo exchanged amused glances. 'Didn't you tell him yet?' Bullock asked.

'No. I thought you ought to be here first.'

'Oh. Well, I guess it's just not your night, Tallis. Somebody just planted a fire-bomb in your apartment. Burned the place out.'

Chapter Seven

Eventually, they stopped asking questions, and left me in a motel room to get some sleep. They let me know that my movements would be watched, but they didn't say why. By that time, I was so tired, I didn't care.

My apartment was a write-off. I doubted whether anything of mine would be even recognizable, let alone worth salvaging. The fire had destroyed half the block, and seriously injured fifteen people. It was an act of savage, blatant destruction; and like everything else that had happened recently, it made no sense at all, though Bullock and Jimbo seemed to detect some pattern in it. Bullock's attitude towards me had changed : he was matier, even a shade patronising, and he behaved as if we shared some slightly disreputable secret. For some reason, I found his new style vaguely disturbing; I felt threatened by it, though I couldn't say why.

The next morning, the first thing I had to do was to shop for shaving-gear and a change of clothes. Two plain-clothes cops followed me all the way, making no attempt to be unobtrusive. They were burly and middle-aged, with faces as tough and shiny as old saddle-leather. Bullock obviously considered me very valuable or very dangerous, to have set these two battle-veterans to watch over me.

Back at the motel, I shaved and changed quickly, and then drove over to St Ann's hospital. On the way, I stopped to buy flowers and fruit. The police car blatantly waited alongside the Lotus until I came out of the shop, and stayed conspicu-

66

ously in my driving mirror for the rest of the trip.

Marje blushed brick-red when I offered her the flowers. I explained what I wanted, and she ushered me into the Casualty Wards with an air of conspiracy that would have aroused suspicion at a hundred yards. No-one paid us any attention except my two watchdogs, who were busying themselves with their two-way radio.

As we walked along the ward, Marje leaned close to me. 'Calls herself Joybelle Jones,' she said in a hoarse, mentholated whisper. 'If you believe that, you'll believe anything.'

In the daylight, and without make-up, the girl looked as defenceless as a baby. Someone had tidied-up her dark hair a little, but her small, thin face was pinched and grey with shock. Her eyes held neither concern nor curiosity: they were as blank as glass beads.

Marje fussed around her, straightening the bedclothes, barking like a sergeant-major. 'Visitor for you, Miss Jones. Gentleman who found you and phoned for the ambulance. Brought you a lovely basket of fruit. Isn't that nice?'

'Great.' Joybelle regarded me listlessly. 'You din' have to worry. I told 'em exactly nothing. What did you expect?'

Marje suddenly stiffened like a gun-dog: one of the burly detectives was peering round the door of the ward. She stalked towards him, rigid with indignation, her hackles rising fearsomely. I turned back to the girl. 'I have to blame myself for what happened to you, Joybelle, I'm sorry.'

'Yeah, I bet you are.' The voice was tight and shrill, but the face revealed nothing. 'You know what them animals did to me? They cut off my nipples, that's what.' Her tears ran down cheeks that might have been carved from wood. 'What kind of a cruddy world is this when people can do that to other people? I wasn't doing 'em any harm.'

I said softly, 'Tell me who they are, Joybelle.'

'Get lost. You think I'm crazy? I'm not telling anybody one single thing, understand? Not ever. Maybe you think I didn't get hurt bad enough? You want me to get my

67

ears cut off next, or my nose, is that it? I had beautiful breasts, mister. Everybody said so.'

'These men have got to be stopped, Joybelle. Don't you want to see them caught?'

'What the hell do I care?'

It was hopeless, but I went on talking : 'The man who was with you last night, the one who tried to protect you—he had some dirty photographs in his wallet. Do you know where he got them?'

She ignored me. 'I wanted to be an actress, you know that? That's why I wanted the money, for voice lessons, dance lessons. I wasn't hurting anybody.'

'You're still young,' I said lamely. 'There's still plenty of time.'

'You're a million laughs, mister,' she said flatly. 'I may split my sides. Better take the fruit with you. It ain't bought you nothing.'

I found Marje in the corridor outside, apparently keeping guard. The two policemen were nowhere to be seen. 'Marje, I'd like to talk to the doctor in charge of Miss Jones. How can I do that?'

'You know him! Dr Bush, the senior consultant. I'll show you to his office.'

It was the same doctor who had attended me. He still looked about nineteen. 'Miss Jones?' he said. 'Physically, the injury isn't too serious. If we needed the bed, we could make out a case for discharging her tomorrow. Mentally and emotionally—well, God knows what damage has been done there.'

'Doctor, I would like this child to have the best care available. Will you advise me as to what that might be?'

He made a steeple of his fingers and considered me gravely. He looked like a sixth-former debating pre-martial sex.

'Money no object?'

'I'll pay whatever it costs.'

'Hm. Excuse me, but what exactly is your interest in

Miss Jones? Why are you taking this trouble?'

'Guilt,' I said simply. 'The girl was on an errand for me when she was assaulted. I feel at least partly responsible.'

'Fair enough. What I will do is to arrange to have her transferred to St Martines's. It's a convalescent home run by nuns. She will have all the privacy she wants, and all the mothering she can cope with. And as soon as it can be arranged, she should have some therapy—something to occupy her whole mind, not give her time to brood.'

'I think you can leave the therapy to me,' I said. 'How soon can you arrange to move her?'

'I'll do it now.' He picked up the telephone. 'Nuns are fantastically efficient. If you would care to leave your phone number on my pad, I'll let you know when she's settled in. Ought to be tomorrow morning.'

Marje walked back with me to the main entrance. 'Thanks for the flowers,' she said. 'I mean it, really. Thanks ever so. It wasn't just so's you could see her, was it?'

'No, Marje. You were very kind to me. I would have brought them in any case.'

'It makes a diff.'

It was my turn to be red-faced. ' 'Bye, Marje,' I said hastily. 'See you.'

'Any time.' She looked wistful. 'Any time.'

The car was as hot as a coke oven inside : by the time I reached Gillian's office my shirt was wringing wet, and my hands were blistered from contact with the steering wheel.

Gillian was not pleased to see me. 'I don't know what the hell you're mixed up in, but I want no part of it,' she rapped. 'I don't even want to hear about it. There's a graveyard stink about you lover, and you look as wholesome and cuddly as a hammerhead shark.'

'This is harmless,' I said soothingly. 'I want you to find me a drama coach. A good one.'

'Some smart fellow offered you a film part?'

'No, this isn't for me. It's for a girl who's in hospital

69

and needs therapy.'

Gillian leered goatishly. 'Gorgeous chick, is she? I guess she's not the only one who needs therapy, hm? Well, you want someone who can do the Prof. Higgins bit on the voice, and help with deportment and so on? As it happens, I do know the ideal guy, but unfortunately for your book, he's as handsome as Paul Newman and as butch as a pedigree bull. You might just find your nose a fraction out of joint.'

'That's fine. Just so long as he's gentle with her. She calls herself Joybelle Jones, but I guess she can be talked out of it. This is the address of the nursing home—' I scribbled on a scrap of paper—'and I'd like him to start tomorrow afternoon, and work with her every day. Ask him to take some books for her, too. I'll pay for them, of course.'

'A five-hundred dollar deposit works swifter than fair words, dear lad. Make a few magic passes over your chequebook before leaving.'

Back in my motel room, dining on sandwiches and beer from a nearby delicatessen, I reflected that whoever had fire-bombed my apartment had probably done me a favour. This room suited me perfectly : it had no memories, no emotional trap-doors. It was just a room; a neat, antiseptic box, as impersonal as a transit camp.

The phone rang, startling me. It was Mick. 'I've had the divil's own job to trace ye,' he boomed. 'Your phone was dead, and I thought you were too, when I read about the fire at your place. What in the name of owd Nick are you up to?'

'Even if I could explain, I wouldn't over this phone, Mick. By now it probably *is* bugged.'

'Ah well, what can you expect, the company you keep. Look, I've been nosing around some after that Johnny Parvo feller, and I'll tell you a funny thing—I learned nothing at all! Not a word out of a soul. Thick-eared rowdies I've known for twenty years, quivering like frightened

70

ould women. One ruffian even told me to be careful. Me!
Better tell me what it's all about, boy I got the feelin' I'm
trying to push around a funnel-web spider with me bare
toe.'

'Mick, you're not going to believe this—'

'Ah, come on! People don't shoot you up and burn your
house down because they don't like your pretty face. Why
won't you trust me?'

'I said you wouldn't believe it. But Mick, you can forget
about Johnny Parvo. That was a mistake. The fellow I saw
was called Ashleaf.'

'Same feller. Johnny Ashleaf. Took the name Parvo when
turned pro. Listen, I can probably find Parvo for you—'

I crossed my thumbs. 'How?'

'Money. Some runty little Judas at the Cross will
open up, if the price is right. How important is it?'

'It's important enough to spend money on, Mick. But
I'm more interested in his friends and acquaintances. See
if you can dig up something on them.'

'Right y'are.'

'Oh, and Mick—you said there was something odd about
him. Did you remember what it was?'

'I did, so. He was jailed for two senseless crimes. One
afternoon, he knocked an old man unconscious, and broke
a little girl's arm. For no reason. In court, they put it down
to the drink, but nobody believes that. The story is that
somebody told him to do it.'

'Paid him, do you mean?'

'No, just told him. Apparently he becomes completely
dependent on the people he calls his friends, to the point of
being their slave, d'ye see?'

I saw. I said slowly, 'That means there's someone behind
Parvo, Mick. Someone manipulating him. That's the one I
want. That's the big fish.'

'Right. I'll toddle off and spend your money for you.'

I remembered something. 'Mick?'

'Yes?'

'What do you know about Carlo's restaurant? Is there something bent going on there? Every time I mentioned the place last night, the cops twittered like bats.'

'Don't ye ever read the papers, ye ignorant poltroon? Nothin' at all's goin' on there: it's been closed for weeks. Somebody gave it the treatment they gave you, boy. They heaved a bomb through the window.' His hoarse chuckle rattled in my ears long after he had rung off.

I sat for a long time, letting my thoughts scurry round and round my brain. Somehow, I had strayed into a mine-field; with every step, some new disaster blew up in my face. I wondered what Archer was doing; and I worried about the unknown man on the phone. They had both threatened me, both demanded something from me. Since I didn't even know what it was, the immediate prospect didn't look too rosy. On top of that, my credibility rating seemed to have sunk to zero. The cops didn't believe me, Mick didn't believe me, Archer and the man on the phone didn't believe me. Even Gillian hadn't bothered to hide her distrust of me.

By nightfall, I was stir-crazy. My thought returned end-lessly to the one sore spot that raged like an aching tooth. The photograph of Helen banished every other image from my mind, became a nagging torment that would give me no peace. I had to get out of that room, do something, anything, to get my mind off that treadmill.

Outside, I looked around for my two watchdogs, but I couldn't see them anywhere. I wasn't sure whether I was glad or sorry about that. They restricted my freedom to some extent, but they also gave me a comforting measure of security. I gave them every chance to catch up with me, driving as circumspectly as a High Court judge; but they still hadn't shown up by the time I parked the car, about a block away from Carlo's. Maybe they had decided to play it subtle for a change. I put the torch from the glove compartment in my pocket, and walked back to the restaurant.

Carlo's had been one of Helen's favourite places in the

city. Only a hundred yards or so off the main tourist strip, it was a small oasis of peace and dignity. It was set back from the narrow street, behind a paved courtyard with high walls on either side. Two bow windows framed a wide, handsome doorway; and the courtyard found room for a fountain, two bay trees in wooden tubs, and a vast honeysuckle which sprawled over a wooden trellis on the right-hand side. I liked the place particularly on summer evenings, when the yellow light from the windows streamed across the paving-stones, and the honeysuckle drenched the night air with its perfume.

There was no light in the courtyard now. The bay trees were dead, the fountain full of rubbish. The blackened window-frames were criss-crossed with planks, and the door had been roughly patched with plywood. There was a heavy padlock hanging from a steel hasp. I looked closely at it. It wasn't holding anything. Someone had unscrewed the staple behind it, and wedged the door shut with a wad of paper. I pushed; the door opened easily and quietly. The darkness beyond it had a sickly, detergent-type smell, mingled with dust and the stink of stale liquor. There was no sound. The crickets suddenly began to chirr in the honeysuckle, emphasising the sense of stillness. When I moved, the sound ceased abruptly, as at the turn of a switch.

I slipped inside, and closed the door behind me before using the torch. The damage was not as great as I had imagined. The fire had gouged an ugly black hole in the right-hand half of the floor, and a couple of scorched tables leaned drunkenly at its edge; but the other side of the room, although indescribably filthy and littered with broken glass and chunks of plaster, was comparatively untouched.

There was a well-defined track of footprints through the litter. It led to a small room that had been a cocktail bar, at the rear of the main restaurant. The feeling of total desolation in the place puzzled me : it seemed out of proportion to the actual damage. The fire looked to have been success-

73

fully contained; a few weeks' work could have set the place to rights. And yet it had just been abandoned; it was odd.

The sickly-sweet smell was almost overpowering in this small room. I could identify it at last : cheap perfume. Some-one had sprayed it everywhere, in an effort to combat the sour smells of damp carpet, nicotine and liquor. The shelves had been cleared; there were only four bottles visible, and they held cheap red candles. The foam-rubber cushions from the wall-benches had been arranged as a crude bed in the centre of the room, and brightly-patterned blankets and scatter-cushions were spread over them, in a pathetic attempt at prettiness. There were girlie magazines and some mildly pornographic photographs on the bar. I felt a sneaking admiration for Joybelle. For an inexperienced, teenage whore, it wasn't a bad attempt at private enterprise.

There was a whisper of movement in the darkness behind me, and something hard and cold jabbed me in the nape of the neck.

My heart froze. A harsh, well-remembered voice said, 'This is a gun, sonny. Do something silly, and make me blow your head off.'

I stayed very still. I didn't want to do anything he might consider silly. Somehow, I knew beyond any doubt that he meant what he said.

Chapter Eight

Archer kept the gun pressed hard against my spine, and searched me carefully for weapons. His hands were trembling, and his breathing was heavy and erratic, as if he had been running hard.

'Put your hands behind your back. Slowly.'

He was not very swift or skilful, getting the handcuffs on me, but I didn't give him any trouble. That gun felt heavy enough to blow my spine to bits.

He circled round me and shone my own torch in my eyes. The light jittered in his hand, dazzling me. Suddenly and without warning, he kicked my feet from under me, and raked the side of my head with the gun barrel as I went down. I sprawled face downwards, and Archer began to kick me brutally and with precision. I was too confused to think quickly; his shoes had thudded into my ribs too many times before it occurred to me to start shouting. That stopped him kicking me at least. He jammed a filthy rag into my mouth, and dragged me into a sitting position against a bench. He held the torch close to my face.

'All right—' Archer could hardly speak; his breath juddered, and the words stuck in his throat. 'Try to understand this, Tallis. It's over, finished. You bloody fool, did you think I'd go down, and not take you with me? You're going to die, you bastard. You're going to die in this greasy stink-hole, for what you did to me and to Mary . . . and the kid. I'm not leaving it to the law. I've seen what your kind do to the law. You and that smooth-faced crud with the

75

swanky yacht—' He twisted his hand in my shirtfront, and shook me in a paroxysm of fury, slamming me hard against the wooden bench. 'Do you know what it was like, trying to find that money, you bloodsucking scab? Or was that part of the fun?'

I tried to spit out the gag. I didn't think he'd listen to me, but I couldn't just sit there and be butchered. He swung the gun at my head again; I managed to catch the main force of the blow on my shoulder, but it knocked me over again. He yanked me upright, helpless as a rag doll. My finger closed around one of the support rails of the bench, and I braced myself for the next assault.

He thrust his face close to mine. 'What the hell did you hope to gain by it? Did you think you'ld save your own lousy skin by destroying me? No, it can't be that. You destroy people because you enjoy it. You had to make sure I had nothing left to live for. Well, neither have you, now. That's the only satisfaction you've left me, Tallis—that you're going first.'

I realized that even if I could get rid of the gag, there was no point in trying to argue with the man. He was beyond the reach of reason; beyond everything perhaps, except the pain of his own private hell. There was a blur of movement behind the dazzle of the torch : he had raised the gun to hit me again. I braced my hands against the wooden framework behind me, and kicked with all my strength. My foot caught his knee, pushing him momentarily off-balance. The gun went off, shockingly close to my head; the heat of the explosion stung my cheek. I rolled sideways and hobbled desperately on my knees towards the bar, diving instinctively for cover. I could hear Archer lumbering after me. My shoulder caught the edge of the bar, and my own momentum jolted me round and sent me staggering backwards. I cannoned into a door in the near wall, and fell through it on my back.

Archer was on me too fast. He tripped over my feet and fell full length on top of me. The gun struck something metallic, and exploded again: the bullet sang like an angry wasp. The recoil must have jerked the gun out of his hand: I heard it clatter onto the floor. The torch had fallen somewhere under our bodies.

I realized that I had to stay close to him to survive. If he reached that gun again, and had space to use it, I was done for. While he fumbled to pick up the torch, I twisted, trapped his hand under my hip, rammed my head into his face with all the force I could muster. It wasn't scientific, but it was effective. It broke his nose. I felt the bone grate against my forehead. Archer cried out, and pulled his head back. I squirmed out from under his weight, kicking like a maniac to keep what initiative I had. My foot connected with the torch; it clanged hollowly against something, and went out. I managed to get clear of him at last, lurched upright, and shuffled feverishly away, like a bear with St Vitus' dance. I was searching for the gun with my feet. The rag in my mouth had come loose in the scuffle; I spat it out, and felt the relief of being able to breathe freely again. The smell, and the metal surfaces everywhere, told me I was in the restaurant's kitchen. I collided with a pile of saucepans and scattered them with a deafening clatter. My foot struck something small and heavy. The gun! I kicked it away as hard as I could; it slid across the floor and ricocheted off another metal surface with a sound like a muffled gong. I couldn't tell where it had gone, and I hoped Archer couldn't, either. But I had lost the initiative, in moving away from him. Even without his gun, he was more than a match for me, while my hands were fastened behind my back. Come to that, I couldn't be sure that he wasn't carrying another gun. I needed luck or an inspiration, or both.

The darkness in here felt constricting, claustrophobic. But—a little pulse of excitement began to beat in my throat —the darkness was not absolute. There was the dim grey silhouette of a narrow strip of window to my right. It was barely distinguishable: a lighter shade of black in the prevailing blackness—but it might be an advantage, if I could

77

figure out how to use it.

I moved backwards, away from the window. My fingers touched a horizontal metal edge, about waist-high. It was some sort of table, or work-bench. I slid my backside onto it, swung my legs up under me, and with an enormous effort, heaved myself upright. My perch wasn't especially precarious, but I had to concentrate hard to keep my balance.

Archer was scrabbling on the floor, hunting for the gun and the torch. He was making quite a lot of noise, but I couldn't be sure he hadn't heard me. If he found the torch, and if it still worked, I was done for, anyway. If not, I had to hope that I had seen the window before he had. Either way, the odds were heavily on his side.

Archer was suddenly still. Had he found something, or was he just listening for me, as I was listening for him? My heart thumped erratically. As the silence lengthened, I became aware of tiny sounds : a tap dripping, the whine of a mosquito, the distant, incredibly ordinary sound of traffic. My heart steadied a little; if he had found the torch, he would have used it. Perhaps the odds had shortened a fraction.

There was another sound. A faint, barely audible whistling, no louder than the mosquito's whine. Archer's nose ! It was broken; he couldn't control that slight wheeze. The noise gave away his position as clearly as a homing signal. For the first time, I began to believe in my chances.

He began to move. Cautiously, feeling his way. I couldn't see him, but I knew where to look for him. I crouched, and fixed my eyes on the outline of the window. The lower edge of the strip of grey light blurred, began to change shape.

I waited until his head was fully silhouetted against the light, and then kicked at the black shape with all the energy I could muster. There was no margin for error: I would only have this one chance. My foot caught him high on the temple, but I couldn't recover my balance; I strode into space and came crashing down on top of him. The

78

fall jarred every bone in my body. I lunged forward at where Archer's head should have been, and rapped my forehead against smooth metal. Stumbling forward, I caught the side of his head with my knee, slamming him against something that boomed like a bass drum. He groaned, and lay still.

I didn't think he was shamming, but I didn't want to stay and find out. I thought briefly of trying to search him for the key to the handcuffs, but I rejected the idea. Even if I could find it, I probably couldn't use it. I had to get out of there. Fast.

I edged away crabwise trying to guide myself through the kitchen by feel. I wasn't sure of my bearings any more, and I didn't know where the door was. Something rolled under my foot; the torch. I knelt down and leaned back on my heels, groping behind me in the dark. I wasted valuable seconds, but I found it at last. It seemed to be broken. I shook it impatiently, and it came on, startlingly bright. The gun wasn't visible anywhere.

Archer lay face downward, not moving. His right arm was hidden underneath his body. I found that I dare not turn my back on him: it suddenly seemed very important to me to know whether or not he held that gun in his right hand. I shone the torch on him and tried to roll him over with my foot, but he was too heavy, in that confined space. I didn't dare waste any more time. As I moved away, my foot caught in his jacket. I shook it free, and something round and shiny fell out of a pocket.

It was another photograph. This one had been savagely crumpled into a ball. I wasted more time in smoothing it out behind my back, the torchlight dancing crazily around the walls. I dropped it on the floor, and bent over it, twisting awkwardly sideways to get some light on it.

This was worse than the other one. Far worse. Helen's face smiled up at me from the creased, glossy print. Helen smiling as I had never seen her smile. Helen naked, her body spread as crudely and as obscenely as only a sick

79

mind could devise. The invitation in her face was as explicit as a textbook of lewdness.

The man with her was Archer. He was naked, except for jackboots and leather wrist bands, and he carried a coiled stock-whip. He ought to have looked ludicrous, but he didn't. Grotesque yes, but not comic. His face was rapt, trance-like, in the grip of an almost religious ecstasy. The shot looked like a still from a film: it was more authentic than the strained artificiality of the usual filthy picture. Even the bruise on her neck, and the lines of the whip-marks across her belly and breasts looked real.

I doubled over, retching painfully. The hammering in my head threatened to pulp my brain. Archer stirred, and began to move, but I didn't care. He had been right all the time: there was nothing left to live for. I wanted to be sick, but I couldn't even achieve that measure of relief. The pain in my throat—and a deeper pain—brought tears to my eyes.

There were other noises, besides the fierce thumping in my head. Shoes crunching over broken glass, doors banging, voices shouting. . . .

Archer was on his knees, mumbling, his head swinging from side to side. The gun dangled limply from his hand. His eyes were wild, unfocussed. I switched off the torch and dived sideways a split second before he fired. The instinct to survive was stronger than my despair, it seemed. I slid across one of the tables, and slumped on the floor on the far side of it.

The voices and the footsteps grew louder. Jimbo's voice, not at all laconic: 'What the hell's going on here?' Then suddenly, a lot of light. I flattened myself to the floor, and crawled a few feet, trying to peer under the bench. If I could see Archer, he could see me. And he was the one with the gun.

Fred's voice: 'It's Merv Archer! He's hurt!'

Jimbo called, 'You all right Merv? What's going on?'

There was too much room for misunderstanding here. I didn't want to be trampled to death by the rescuing cavalry.

I croaked from the floor: 'For God's sake, take that gun off him!'

'Who's that?' The torch lights bobbed erratically round the room.

'It's me, Tallis. That madman's trying to kill me.'

'All right.' The drawl was back in Jimbo's voice; he had the situation under control. 'There are three police officers in this room, Tallis. Just throw your gun out here, and get up nice and slow.'

It was turning into farce, but I didn't feel like laughing at all. 'I don't have a gun, and my hands are fastened behind my back.' I hoped he believed me: it didn't sound plausible, even to me. 'And I'm not coming out while he's still got that gun. He's a maniac!'

There was a pause while Jimbo considered this. 'Better put the gun away, Merv,' he said at last. 'He can't escape the three of us.'

Archer made no reply. I rested my cheek against the greasy floor, and wished I could see what was going on. Suddenly the full beam of one of the torches caught me. Fred had moved silently round the side of the bench.

'Hey, it's true!' he shouted. 'This bloke's trussed up like a frozen chook. He's—'

But I was already on the move. I had seen what Archer saw a microsecond later: the bench was protecting only my head and shoulders; my belly and legs were clearly in the line of fire. The shot ricocheted deafeningly into a stack of saucepans. I took shelter behind a large stove. It looked solid enough; I hoped it was.

'Christ!' breathed someone into the awestruck silence. 'Christ!'

'Hold it, Merv,' Jimbo commanded tersely. 'Just hold it right there. Drop the gun.'

Archer still said nothing. I couldn't see him. The only one I could see was Fred, whose mouth hung open in an idiot mask of astonishment.

Jimbo's voice, deliberately calm: 'We came out looking

81

for you, Merv, as soon as we learned you had taken over from the men watching Tallis. Nobody told you to do that, did they? We got worried about you. We spotted Tallis's car, and a little later, we heard the shooting in here, and—'

Archer interrupted him, his voice a hoarse whisper. 'Mary's dead.'

'What?'

'I said Mary's dead. And the kid. That bastard killed them.'

Jimbo said tensely, 'How do you know?'

'I know.'

'But—'

'Stop shining that light at me!' Archer shouted. 'Why can't you leave me alone?'

'Put the gun down, Merv.'

Archer's teeth began to chatter. 'He's not fit to live. You don't understand. He's got to die.'

'Cool it!' Jimbo snapped. 'We'll take him round to the station house and charge him. We'll just do it by the book. However sure you are, you don't do the judge and jury bit, Merv. Not ever.'

'I'm going to kill him,' Archer said.

'No you're not, Merv. Not unless you shoot me first. And I don't believe you'ld do that.'

'I shall if I have to. Keep away!'

I peered carefully round the edge of the stove. Archer was on his feet now, facing Jimbo. He was shaking as though he had a fever, and trying to hold the gun steady with both hands.

Jimbo sighed, and put his torch down on a table. 'You have to hand over the gun, Merv,' he said gently. 'Cops don't shoot their friends. And we're wasting time.'

Archer retreated a step. 'Keep back!' he rasped. 'If you knew what he was, what he's done, you'ld help me to kill him. Don't get in my way, copper. I swear I'll shoot you down if you come any closer!'

Jimbo shrugged. 'Okay,' he said casually. 'You'ld better

get it over with, so's we'll both know what it's like.'

He put out his hand, like a man offering food to a dog, and stepped forward. The gun danced in Archer's trembling hand, pointed menacingly at Jimbo's chest. Jimbo smiled wanly. He stopped when his hand was about a foot away from the gun, and waited unmoving, relaxed. Archer's hands were shaking uncontrollably now; he sobbed and made inarticulate animal sounds. He struck the air with his fist: a meaningless, futile gesture. Then he reversed the gun, put the muzzle into his mouth, and blew off the top of his head.

Chapter Nine

There were four cops in the interrogation-room: Jimbo, Bullock, Fred, and one I'd never seen before. The newcomer was a Scotch-terrier of a man, small and fierce with bristling eyebrows and moustache. The tension in the room was like the build-up to a thunderstorm. No-one believed my story, not even the parts that were true.

Bullock had said nothing so far. He sat on a chair behind the others, his jolly farmer's face lined and sagging.

Scotch-terrier was unable to sit still. He paced up and down, snapping questions and worrying at his lower lip with his teeth. Now, he paused in front of my chair and clasped his hands behind his back. 'All right, all right!' he barked, dismissing everything I'd said so far. 'How long had you been blackmailing Detective Archer?'

'Don't be such a bloody fool,' I said wearily. If he was trying to irritate me, he had succeeded. 'I wasn't blackmailing anybody.'

'Archer obviously believed you were,' Jimbo commented gently. 'How do you account for that?'

'Archer was nuts. That picture proves it, and his actions tonight prove it. How many more psychos have you got on the payroll?'

I had rattled them, and their faces showed it. Scotch-terrier was the first to recover. 'You can't bullyrag your way out of this one, Tallis. This caper stinks like a dead goat. It don't take a genius to figure it out. You and the Simons woman had a blackmail set-up; she's the bait, you

84

take bedroom photos with a concealed camera. It ain't new, but it's nifty, if you can work it. Only with Archer, you got a bonus. He's not only kinky, he's a cop. Now, there's a situation full of possibilities. How many others did you trap, Tallis? How many pathetic little perves did she strip down for? She looks as if she had a talent for it, I'll say that much.'

'Shut up!'

'Don't get righteous with me, Tallis. You're up to the dandruff in this stinking mess. You didn't get a fancy apartment and an expensive car out of a house-wrecker's pay. And what about that wad of loot we found at Simon's place?' He paused, aware of having scored a point, and waited for my reaction before pressing on: 'The caper came unstuck, as it was bound to do, because it had a fatal flaw: the girl had to be out in the open. The mugs knew *her* face all right. Sooner or later, someone would trace the link between you. And that's exactly what happened. Some other poor bastard you had put through the mangle tracked you down by way of that girl, and was desperate enough to try to murder you in the street.'

'Archer wasn't the gunman in the van?' I asked quickly.

Scotch-terrier stopped pacing. 'Now, that's a thought—?'

Bullock spoke for the first time. 'No it isn't,' he said heavily. 'Merv Archer was with me at that time.'

'Anyway—' the little man attacked again—'You admit he had a motive for killing you?'

'No, but he might have thought he had,' I said. 'He might have jumped to the same conclusions you have.'

Scotch-terrier ignored that. He started pacing again. 'Okay, so another blackmail victim did the shooting. Archer was called in on the case. He pieced the whole thing together, the moment he saw the dead girl; and every bit of later evidence—the money in her flat, the cameras in yours—pointed the same way. He phoned you—he wanted the money back, for starters. But you had to play it stupid. You sent those photographs to his home, to his wife. God knows what you thought you'ld achieve by that.' Again he waited for my reaction. 'I'll tell you what you did achieve: you wiped out a whole family. Those pictures drove Mary Archer insane. She left a note for her husband, and then smothered her child in its cot before poisoning herself with household ammonia. Can you imagine the agony of despair that would drive a woman to do that?'

He wasn't looking for a comment this time, but I made one anyway. 'I never knew Archer, or his family. But I know one thing: there's one piece of evidence you've shoved under the carpet—Archer was insane. I'm sorry about his wife and child, but I am not, repeat not, responsible for their deaths, directly or indirectly. I did not send any photographs to her home.'

'Then who did?'

'I don't know.'

'It had to be someone who knew Simons, right?'

'I suppose so.'

'We've checked with Miss Simons's office and with her neighbours; everybody says she had no regular men-friends other than you. Is that right?'

'I don't know.'

'She never mentioned any other man, in all the time you knew her?'

'I knew I wasn't the first man in her life, if that's what you mean. But it wasn't something we needed to talk about.'

'So you can't give us the name of a single one of her previous boy friends?'

'No.'

'Exactly. So we're stuck with you, Tallis.'

Now, I was really angry. 'That's the stupidest piece of chop-logic I've ever heard! There's not a shred of evidence against me, other than my connection with Helen Simons, and you know it. You're convinced that I am guilty, because I'm the only one you can see.'

Jimbo smiled thinly. 'Nine times out of ten, the one we

86

can see, is the one we want.'

'Not this time, buster.'

Scotch-terrier bounced back into the fray. 'You want evidence?' he yapped at me. 'The lab boys are working on it right now. We know that these photographs of Archer and the Simon woman were taken with a movie camera. We aim to prove they were taken with the same camera we salvaged from your flat, this morning.'

I gaped at him. Even if what he suggested were possible, which I doubted, no movie camera could have survived in working order, after that fire. He had to be desperate, to try a bluff like that. I stood up.

Scotch-terrier bristled some more. 'Where do you think you're going?'

'I just decided not to co-operate any more,' I said. 'If you want to play it pig-headed, let's do it your way. Charge me, or let me go.'

'You're not going anywhere!'

'Am I under arrest?'

'You're being detained for questioning. We'll arrest you when we're ready.'

'If I'm being detained at all, I have the right to complain to my Embassy about this harassment.' I didn't know whether that was true, but it gave them something to think about. 'If I'm being charged, get on with it. Let's get in court, and talk about how a police officer handcuffed an unarmed prisoner, and then tried to shoot him. And maybe throw in a few words about some interesting photographs of that trusted public servant.'

They digested that in silence, apart from some heavy breathing. Jimbo whistled. 'He's right, Mac,' he said. 'The Press would crucify us. Everybody collects, when that kind of shit hits the fan.'

Scotch-terrier glared at him, and then back at me. 'You watch your mouth, Tallis, or I'll—' Jimbo touched him on the arm and he stopped abruptly. 'Wait here,' he barked, and marched out of the room, stiff-backed. The others trooped silently after him.

A few minutes later, Bullock returned with a photographer, who posed me against a blank wall for mug-shots. While the man fiddled with his lamps. Bullock said thoughtfully, 'There's a dent in the bonnet of your car, John. Run into something?'

The use of my first name threw me more than the question. I hesitated, suspecting a trap. Had Parvo's body been found, and did Bullock suspect my involvement? If he caught me out in a really clumsy lie, they'd probably lock me up and lose the key. However, I didn't have much choice, in the circumstances. 'Parking-lot scars,' I said. 'Never even saw it happen.'

'Tough.' He sounded as if his mind was busy elsewhere. The photographer finished and packed up his gear. Fred came back, caught Bullock's eye, and shrugged.

'So what's the verdict?' I asked. 'Can I go now?'

Bullock sighed. 'Oh, there was never much doubt about that. The Super was impressed, I could tell. Sure, you can go. There are just one or two formalitities first.'

'Such as what?'

'Well, now—' Bullock scratched his head. 'There's a persistent smell of sudden death about you, John; and none of us know where it's coming from. We're going to put you under the microscope.'

It seemed he was talking literally. They escorted me to a small clinic, where two men in white coats took samples of my hair, sweat, saliva, blood, and the dirt under my finger-nails. They went over my clothes with a small vaccum-cleaner, and scraped the dust off my shoes into buff envelopes, one for each shoe. When the men in white coats were satisfied that they had collected enough trophies, I was taken back to the interrogation-room and questioned until everybody was hoarse and bad-tempered. Finally, they said I could go home, and provided transport back to my car.

Back at the motel, a sleepy desk-clerk handed me a note.

A Miss Joybelle Jones had phoned and asked me to contact her. It would have to wait; it was nearly three o'clock in the morning. I was so tired, I nearly fell asleep in the shower. I wrapped a couple of bath-towels round me, and just made it to the bed before I passed out.

Next day, I woke up late, had breakfast in my room, and tried to phone Mick. He wasn't home. I called the nursing-home and asked for Joybelle. She sounded breathless and shy. 'Can I see you? I mean, I want to say thank you an' that. You don't know what it means, you can't. . . . And that Jeremy! He's a drama teacher? Oh, wow!'

'You don't need to thank me, Joybelle. Just concentrate on getting better.'

'No, but can I see you—soon? Please? I can't say everything on the phone.'

'All right,' I said. 'I'll be over as soon as I'm shaved and dressed.'

I tuned in to the radio news. Johnny Parvo's body had been washed up on a North Shore beach, but the police were waiting for an autopsy report before making any comment. There was no mention of his car.

Just before leaving for the nursing-home, I phoned Gillian's office. 'Gill? I thought you'ld like to know that the drama coach you provided is a great success. Just what was wanted.'

'Trust your auntie to provide only the best, Johnny. That Jeremy's terriffic. Good actor, too. Glad you're pleased.'

'If you need to contact me, I'm at the Starbird Motel.' I gave her the phone number.'

'Yeah.' Gillian seemed to be debating something with herself. 'Look, I've been thinking about that other thing you asked—about that blonde chick, the dancer. Maybe I can help after all. You want to look at some photos?'

'Thanks, Gill. I'll be round sometime this afternoon.'

The motel car-park was a narrow rectangle of asphalt,

with a high wattle fence along its northern side. There were not many cars on the lot: the Lotus stood conspicuously apart from the rest, looking as battered and begrimed as if it had just finished a cross-country safari. Two men leaned in the shade of the fence, smoking. Bullock had obviously put his guard-dogs back on duty.

The two men threw away their cigarettes and sauntered over as I unlocked the car. They wore dark glasses and floppy linen sun-hats. The young, slim one was in a monogrammed shirt and tailored slacks. He had a golden chain round his neck, and a thick gold bangle round his wrist. The middle-aged one wore a creased brown suit, and looked like a circus bear that had slipped its chain.

'Excuse me,' the young one said, in a high clear voice. 'Mr John Tallis?'

'Yes?' I turned to face them.

'We have a message for you.'

They moved in swiftly and methodically, converging from each side and forcing me back against the car. They used their fists scientifically and in perfect understanding with each other: this was clearly a routine they had rehearsed many times. The young one aimed a hook at my head; as I flinched away, the other caught me with a beautifully-timed jab under the heart that brought tears to my eyes. Brown-suit had both my arms pinned behind my back before I had time to catch my breath. The whole attack had lasted less than five seconds.

The slim one smiled, and leaned a heavily-ringed hand against my chest. 'Ricky's mad with you, little friend. He said to bring a wad of lettuce down to his boat last night, remember? He sent us around to jog your memory.' He cuffed my face, half-playfully. One of his rings cut my lip.

It promised to be a bad scene; I braced myself to meet it. But it was over sooner than I expected.

'Hey!' Someone shouted from the far end of the car-park. 'Hey! What's going on there?' A young man in jeans and a denim shirt started to run towards us. The thugs pushed me over the bonnet of my car, and took off without another word. They disappeared round the corner of the motel. The young man helped me to my feet, took a few steps after the two men, then turned back, looking irresolute. He was a tall, wide-shouldered boy, with a mane of yellow hair. His forehead and the tip of his nose were painfully sunburnt. 'Are you all right, sir? Do you want a doctor or something? Or the police?' His voice had a plangent, nasal twang: an accent I'd never heard before.

'No, don't trouble,' I gasped. 'I'll be okay in a minute.' I hoped so, anyway. The bruise under my ribs scalded like an over-hot poultice.

'Muggers, were they?' His blue eyes shone. 'Did they get anything?'

'No, you turned up just in time. Thanks.'

'We ought to call the police.'

'Yes,' I said. 'Maybe I will.'

'Well—' He suddenly looked awkward, at a loss. 'If you're sure you're all right—?'

'Quite sure. And thanks again.'

'Nothing to it.' He began to edge away. 'Oh—you wouldn't be the manager of this place, would you? I'm looking for a vacation job?'

'No, sorry.'

'It doesn't matter. Plenty of jobs around, at Christmas-time.' He waved a hand cheerily, and left me. I drove thoughtfully over to St Martine's nursing-home, massaging my bruised ribs with my fist.

Joybelle's room was bright with sunshine, and smelled of flowers and new books. She was sitting up in bed, surrounded by magazines and scraps of notepaper, chattering animatedly into a bedside telephone. She blushed when she saw me, chirped an incoherent farewell to her caller, and rang off. 'That was Jeremy. He wanted to come round before lunch, but I told him I had to see you first.' She stretched out her hands to me, and I sat on the edge of her bed.

'You're looking better already, Joybelle.' It was true. Her

91

hair was brushed and shining; there was colour in her cheeks and liveliness in her eye. But the biggest change of all was the happiness that radiated from her like the heat from a flame.

'Jeremy says I have an ear! For speech, that is. That's a great talent, he says. Not everyone has it. He says I can do anything I want to, if I believe in myself. He says I've got to soak things up like a sponge, read and study, and. . . .' She hiccupped and began to cry, hanging on to my hands as if they were her last hope. 'Oh, Mister, you don't know what it means to me. What can I say?'

'Don't say anything, kid.' I grinned at her. 'Just get well.'

'No, but there is one thing. The things you wanted to know—'

I cut in brusquely. 'Forget it. That's all in the past. It has nothing to do with your life from now on.'

'Yes, it has!' She looked fierce. 'I didn't think I'd need to explain it to you, of all people. I wasn't afraid of those bastards until they hurt me, and then I was so afraid, I would have licked their boots to please them. That's what real fear does to you, Mister. It turns you into a dog.'

'Did Jeremy tell you that, too?'

'Nossir, I worked that out for myself. And as long as I go on being afraid, I'll go on being a dog. A dog don't deserve the friends I got.' She squeezed my hands and went on more calmly, 'Now don't interrupt, just listen. I'll say it only once, and only to you. The protection caper at the Cross and a couple of other districts, is run by a man called Rick Lucy. He operates in just one field: prostitution. His rules are quite simple: every girl on the game pays her dues every week or she gets the treatment. The treatment comes in two doses. First, a warning—like they handed out to me—and if you ignore that, something much worse, like knee-capping, or losing an eye.'

Her matter-of-factness took my breath away. 'How old are you, Joybelle?'

'What does that matter? Old enough. I been around.

Now, this Rick Lucy, he don't dirty his hands hisself. There's Bev and Polly, for instance, the apes that razored me. Bev is about twenty-five, dresses and talks like a queen; the one they call Polly is about twenty years older; a fat, greasy pig.' She shuddered.

I didn't tell Joybelle that I had made the acquaintance of Bev and Polly less than an hour ago; she had enough on her mind. 'Any others?' I asked.

'I've only seen one other. A little guy with glasses and real long hair. I don't know his name. But they say the real heavies are called Johnny and the Dancer. I've never seen them and I don't want to. They're killers.'

'How do you know that? Is there any proof?'

She shrugged. 'Who needs proof? Fear is what these boys trade in. That's why they'll never get caught, see? Who'll be a witness against them? Who wants to be shark-bait? There's a helluva lot of ocean out there.'

'And Rick Lucy has a yacht,' I nodded thoughtfully.

'So you do know about him? I never told you that!' Her eyes widened in shock. 'Oh Christ!'

'What's the matter?'

'I just remembered something,' she whispered. She took her hands from mine and pressed them against her cheeks. 'They say the Dancer is one of the biggest blokes you've ever seen. And he talks with an American accent.'

Chapter Ten

'Don't you start,' I said irritably. 'The cops have already chased up that blind alley. Now I understand why.'

'I'm sorry. The idea sort of took me by surprise. It's too ridiculous.' But the shadow lingered. 'What are you going to do?'

'I don't know. Talk to a few more people, I guess.' I caught the look of apprehension in her eyes. 'Don't worry; I shan't involve you. I promise.'

'Thanks.' She shivered in spite of the heat, and plucked at the bedclothes. 'There was that other thing you wanted to know—about the photos.'

'That's right. Do you know who took them?'

'No, but I'm sure the Lucy mob have nothing to do with that racket. It's strictly small-time stuff.'

'Where did you get them?'

'Where everybody else does. These two drag queens at the Sloppy Dog Club have practically cornered the porn market. Ran it as a sideline, and gradually built it up by strong-arming the competition out of business.'

'Names?'

'Phil and Jimmy. I don't know their second names. They call themselves Phyllis and Jenny in the show. Now, don't go messing around with them. Mister. They may dress up as women, but don't be fooled. They're tough and they're nasty.'

'I'll bear it in mind, Joybelle. Thanks.'

'Well—' she looked coy—'I don't know that I'll call myself Joybelle any more. Jeremy thought I ought to go for some-

94

thing a bit more classy. Something like Jane, perhaps.'

'Jane's nice,' I said. 'Jane Jones?'

'No, I wanted something with real tone. I was thinking, maybe . . . Jane Seymour. What do you think?'

'Very appropriate. She was a very brave lady, too.'

The heat and humidity had built up steadily all day, and Gillian was obviously suffering. She was barefoot, every button on her cotton dress seemed to be undone, and she was sitting in the full draught of a large electric fan. The papers on her desk rattled and snapped like flags in the breeze, and were anchored down by books, ashtrays and one of her sandals.

'Thought you weren't going to make it,' she growled, handing me a small sheaf of glossy prints. 'Hurry it up, lover: I'm melting before your very eyes, and liable to trickle through the floorboards at any second.'

The topmost print showed the girl I was looking for. There was no mistaking that platinum hair. The scrawl on the back of the sheet said 'Virginia Crewe, 5ft 4in, Classical-Modern.' There was no address.

I handed the print to Gillian. 'Tell me about this one.'

'Ginny? Good dancer. Works regularly on the Ron Blood Show, Channel O; and they're top-rating. They can afford the best.'

'Does she make a lot of money at that?'

'For a hoofer, sure.'

'Enough to let her spend, say, eight hundred dollars on a dress?'

'You're crazy! This is a rank-and file kid.'

'Gillian, you know everything about everybody, so you can tell me this: was this girl involved in any criminal activity?'

She hesitated. 'Well, there's always gossip . . . but, no. No, I never heard of anything specific. To be honest, I don't think she has the brains for anything but hoofing.'

'All the same, she was getting money from somewhere,

Gill. Maybe she has a sugar-daddy? Or some rich boy-friend?'

Gillian barked with laughter. 'Don't let those baby-blue eyes fool you, Johnny. This girl is one of the city's best-known, adept and practising lesbians.'

The sight of my cheque-book persuaded Gillian to provide me with Virginia Crewe's address, and I wasted the next few sweltering hours in establishing that Virginia didn't live there any more. In fact she hadn't lived there for years. Nor did the present owner of the flat have any forwarding address. I checked in the phone book: there was no entry under her name. I had reached another dead end.

The sun had gone down, but the air was still uncomfortably hot and damp. I went back to the motel, showered and changed. The new clothes felt stiff and oppressive.

I didn't appear to be in great demand, socially. There were no messages for me; Mick still didn't answer his phone; no policemen or hoodlums loitered in the car park. I called a cab and went back to the Cross.

The Sloppy Dog Club was at the end of a narrow alley off Bayswater Street. It was new, but it didn't look permanent. Fresh paint had been carelessly daubed over blistered and peeling woodwork, the carpet in the foyer was thin and cheap, and the gaudy wallpaper was already curling at the edges. Life-size posters of drag-queens flanked a sleazy box-office, where a lank-haired girl crouched over a looking-glass, examining a fine crop of pimples on her upper lip. Yes, she said, Phil and Jenny were in the show. No, she couldn't give them a message, or suggest how I might get in touch with them. The last show finished about 2.30 a.m. Still without looking up from her mirror, she suggested that I might like to book for dinner and the second show?'

I was hungry, but I wasn't so desperate as to eat in a dump like that. I walked round to Mother's Cellar, and drank a vodka martini while Mother fixed up a steak and salad. The drink and the meal were both up to the restaurant's aristocratic standards. Fortified, I lingered over the coffee and tried to fit some of the pieces of the puzzle together.

Two facts stood out: Helen had been involved in a pornography and blackmail racket; and one of her killers was an ex-pug called Johnny Parvo. There was a 'heavy' in Rick Lucy's gang called Johnny. Was it the same man? Was the 'Dancer' the other man I was hunting? There were too many possible answers; a murky sort of pattern was emerging, but there were too many gaps to make a coherent picture of it: too many questions still to be answered. The most nagging question of all: who had actually taken those photographs? Less important, but equally puzzling: why hadn't Helen's parents come forward? Or her husband? There was something else, too—another odd circumstance that I had meant to investigate further, but I couldn't remember what it was. It lurked maddeningly at the edge of my memory, just refusing to materialize. I put it out of my mind: it would return when it was ready, and in the meantime I had plenty to think about.

The horrors of the last few days had granted me just one dispensation of mercy: Helen's image had become blurred in my mind. Or, more accurately, I had made two separate people of her. The woman I had loved stayed blessedly aloof from the dissolute bitch of the photographs; the woman who now showed me a new face of evil at every new turn of events, was a stranger to me. 'My' Helen was untouched by all the filth that now clung to her ghost. The constriction around my heart eased a little; I felt lighter in spirit, as if some crisis had been passed.

There was a snapshot of Helen in my wallet. I studied it carefully, looking in that face for a sign of the viciousness I now knew to be there. But if the signs were there, I couldn't read them. Every detail of her face was as dear to me as it had ever been. I could feel no anger or indignation, only a sense of loss that made my throat ache. I put the snapshot into my jacket pocket, and trudged out into the night to dig up some more filth.

The Stage-door of the Sloppy Dog Club was at the rear

of the building, in a small yard cluttered with refuse-bins and cardboard boxes. It was not an attractive door. Every square inch of it was decorated with obscene and unimaginative slogans; and the naked light bulb dangling above was almost obliterated by its attendant swarm of moths and mosquitoes. A cat-sized rat rootled nonchalantly among the litter.

The door was not locked, and there was no stage-door-keeper. In fact, there was nowhere for a stage-doorkeeper to be. Just a short, narrow corridor, and another door. The further door opened onto another corridor, at right angles to the first, but just as narrow, and just as empty. A hand-painted sign pointed left, to the stage. I could hear taped music, background stuff: this was probably an interval.

There were several doors to the right. One of them opened, and the corridor was suddenly raucous with screeches and guffaws. A gorgeous redhead teetered towards me, in high heels and a sequined bikini.

'Hel-lo, sailor!' The voice was a husky baritone. 'Who's naughty, then? Look girls, a naughty sailor, come ashore to get his funnel scraped!'

Faces appeared at the door: pink-and-white faces, with scarlet lips and incredibly perfect hair-styles. Strident voices in chorus: 'Oh Gawd, another bloody freak!' An exquisite little brunette complained bitterly: 'Why doesn't that drunken old piss-artist ever lock that effing door?'

The redhead sauntered closer. 'What's your fancy, sailor?' There was heavy stubble under the floury-white powder on her chin, and the pale blue eyes, under the false lashes, were bleak and hostile. Other 'girls' crowded into the corridor, bringing with them a smell compounded of stale sweat, cigarette-smoke and cheap perfume. I had a confused impression of feathers, frills, bows, and smooth-shaven legs in nylon tights. And eyes, above all: wide, confident, staring eyes, black-circled with mascara and freakish eyelashes.

I said, 'I'd like a quick word with Phil and Jimmy.'

The redhead smiled thinly, and stuck out a padded hip. 'I'm Jenny, sailor. What's the proposition?' Her eyes flicked sideways.

I turned, but too late. A hand the size of a bear's paw grabbed my shoulder, spun me round, and slammed me against the wall. A creature in a fuzzy Afro-wig, black panties and a padded bra towered over me. She had soft, rounded features, little piggy eyes, and the shoulders of a heavyweight boxer. 'Hi!' she grunted.

I guessed it was Phil, but I didn't return her greeting, because she had my throat clamped in one hand, and a pair of wickedly-pointed scissors in the other.

Chapter Eleven

'Hokay, stickybeak,' Phil said. 'Let's make with the quick word.'

One of the girls tittered. 'How about Goodbye?' she suggested. 'Or, Help!?'

Even with the wig and fancy underwear, no-one could mistake Phil for a woman, at this range. He was big and muscular and dangerous. Without the heels, he wouldn't really be much taller than I was; but he wouldn't be any shorter, either. At the moment, he looked about as appealing as a witch-doctor shopping around for a human sacrifice.

The red-head edged closer. 'I bet this is the snooper old Slaggy Annie warned us about.'

'The Box-office Bombshell?'

'Yeah. Don't waste much time, does he?'

Phil pressed me hard against the wall, clicking the scissors ominously close to my left ear. I relaxed against the pressure. He wanted to show me how strong he was. He was pretty strong. 'Come on, snooper,' he growled. 'Let's hear the quick word.'

He was playing for laughs; I couldn't speak with that grip on my throat, and he knew it. 'You're a trespasser, do you know that? One of those weirdos who sneak in here off the street, looking for quick feel-up. We know your sort. We have to protect ourselves from weirdos and perverts like you.'

Jimmy cooed, 'But darling, don't you think the gentleman

ought to tell us who he is?' Without warning, he short-armed me viciously in the ribs. 'And why he's been asking questions about us, as if we were just a couple of cheap tarts?'

'Tell you what, lovely,' grinned Phil. 'I'm going to let go of his windpipe so's he can tell us all those things. No, you don't have to nudge him again. He seems quite reasonable. Hasn't tried to be physical at all, you notice.' He eased the grip on my throat, and splayed his big hand on my chest, 'So what's it all about, blue-eyes?'

I massaged my throat gingerly. 'It's about this girl,' I croaked. I showed them my photograph of Helen. 'You've been selling pictures of her to some of your clients. Sex pictures. I want to know who took the photographs, and where you got them.'

Phil and Jimmy looked at each other and raised finely-pencilled eyebrows. The feathered and bewigged chorus behind them stirred, became tense. 'Oh, naughty old sly-boots!' breathed Jimmy. His pale eyes were unnaturally bright. 'Whatever will you say next?'

The relentless camp nagged at my nerves. 'I won't shop you,' I said wearily. 'I want the information for my own reasons. Nothing to do with the law.'

'You ought to say please, you know.' Phil gave me another shake. 'Must be polite. If you're a rude little weirdo, I shall have to slap your wrist.'

'Okay,' I said mildly. 'Please?'

Jimmy giggled. 'Isn't he sweet?'

Phil twisted his hand in my shirt, just like the tough guy in the movies. 'We don't know anything about any filthy pictures, see? And we don't dig spies and snoopers. You come snooping around again, and I'll tear off your arm and beat out your brains with it.'

'I think,' I said slowly, 'that it's time you took your hands off me, big-mouth.'

'Ooh!' shrieked Jimmy, 'you're so beautiful when you're angry!'

101

Phil showed his capped white teeth in a tight grin, and scraped his fingernails lightly across my cheek. 'Doesn't little creep like being leaned on? Mustn't whinge, little creep, or Auntie will have to teach you a lesson.'

Out of the corner of my eye, I saw Jimmy move in closer for his favourite short-arm jab. I guessed I was about to be worked over. The Feather-and bracelets brigade shuffled about, straining for a better view. This was the big feature.

They were both playing to the gallery too much, or maybe they were simply over-confident. Either way, they were criminally careless. I took Phil's hand in my right, and swung it outwards and down, pulling hard against the elbow lock, and turning swiftly to increase the momentum. In those heels, Phil never had a chance. He crashed into Jimmy, pinning him against the wall. I had Phil in the old-fashioned judo grip now, with both my thumbs pressed into the back of his hand. I forced his hand back against his forearm, and pulled him towards me, still moving in a tight circle. I heard a scream; the scissors Phil was holding had made an ugly gash in Jimmy's right thigh, and blood was already flowing over his flesh-coloured tights. Phil's woolly head hit the wall, and he slid face downward onto the floor. He moaned, as much from surprise as pain. The whole thing had taken less than ten seconds: his mind hadn't yet caught up with events.

I put my foot on his neck, and braced his elbow against my leg. I could control him easily with one hand now. I used the other to feint hard at Jimmy, who was reaching over Phil's body, apparently to scratch my eyes out. I pulled the punch fractionally short of his snub nose, and he reared back from my fist like a terrified horse, his blue eyes dilating with fright.

'My *face*!' he breathed. 'You nearly hit my *face*!'

Somebody giggled nervously.

I said harshly, 'You didn't have to play it tough. Particularly as you don't have the talent for it. Now, where

102

did you get those photographs, and who took them?'

'Get lost,' mumbled Phil. Game to the last.

'You can't frighten us, you bully!' sobbed Jimmy. He was plainly terrified. 'Somebody phone for the law!' He fumbled in the top of his bikini, took out a filthy wad of cotton-wool and tried to staunch the bleeding from his thigh. Phil released the scissors, and thumped his fist feebly on the floor. He was weakening fast; his back was beaded with sweat, and he was panting irregularly.

'Last chance, Phil,' I said. 'Which shall I break first, your finger, or your wrist?'

'Jesus Christ!' one of the queens said in an awe-struck whisper. 'He means it, the sod. He really means it!'

'Don't be too hard on him, Phil!' someone called, and the girls tittered like the junior girls' assembly.

Phil moaned, and tried to twist his head away from me. 'Help me, you stupid tarts!' he gasped. 'For God's sake, help me!'

Nobody moved. Apart from Jimmy, nobody showed any expression at all, other than a beady curiosity. I increased the pressure on Phil's fingers, and he began to whimper like a frightened puppy. It was Jimmy who capitulated, however. 'Stop it, stop it!' he cried, 'all right, so we sold a few pictures, what's the harm? Why can't you leave us alone?'

'Who took the photographs?'

'We don't know. Honest to God, I swear we don't know.'

'How about it, Phil?' I asked.

'It's true, honest. . . . Let go of me, I won't give you any strife. Please?'

I relaxed the pressure, but I kept him where he was. Jimmy said, 'We get the Heidi photos from a kid in the business, like us. But she doesn't take the pictures; she's just like an agent, see?'

'Heidi?'

'That's the name of the model. I don't know whether it's her real name. The stuff's local, so I guess she is. But

103

I never met her.'

'So who's the supplier?'

'Her name's Virginia Crewe. She's a dancer.'

I felt a stab of excitement. The ends were coming together at last. 'Address?'

'I don't know exactly. She kept it a secret. Her phone number's not listed, even. But heard she lived up in Collaroy.'

One of the chorus said unexpectedly, 'She has a beachside bungalow up there. You can't mistake it: it's all white except for a door-knocker like a pair of red ballet-shoes. Dead naff, if you ask me.'

'How do you know she lives there?' I asked.

'Because I've seen her there. I recognized her from the Ron Blood Show.'

I looked back at Jimmy. 'How do you contact her?'

'We don't. When she has some stuff, she gets in touch with us.'

I let go of Phil, who sprawled on the floor, holding his injured hand between his thighs. 'You going to make trouble?' he mumbled.

'Not unless this is a bum steer,' I said. 'If it is, I'll be back to snap your garter.'

The little group watched me go in silence, shuffling their feet and nervously adjusting greasy straps and tatty jewellery. Nobody threw anything, not even a kiss.

Chapter Twelve

I was on the road before eight o'clock the next morning, but the coolest part of the day was already over. Heat shimmered over the long queues of cars flowing into the city; sunlight bounced blindingly off metal and glass and blue water. Hundreds of small craft bobbed at each side of Middle Harbour Bridge, their rainbow sails peacocking against the silver dazzle of the sea. The Lotus' wheels drummed briefly on the metal surface of the bridge, then headed towards the coast road, a wide dusty track with little drifts of sand in the gutters. Limitless, achingly blue sky, and glimpses of limitless blue sea. And the sun-bleached signs of the authentic Australia: Coca-cola, hamburgers, Kentucky-fried chicken.

There is a lot of beach at Collaroy. And, although the best sites are being remorselessly gobbled up by the locust-plague of motels, there are a lot of bungalows that might claim to be beach-side. However, I found the one I sought very quickly. Its very neatness made it conspicuous, and its whiteness struck the eye like a blow. The weatherboard walls were white, and the fence around the bare, paved yard. Even the curtains were white. The only contrast was the doorknocker in the shape of a pair of ballet-shoes, bright scarlet against the gleaming front door.

Nobody answered my knock, and there were no sounds of movement inside the bungalow. The curtains at some of the windows were closed; maybe Virginia was a late riser. She was in show-business, after all. I resigned myself to a long wait.

The car was already much too hot for comfort. I parked it in a patch of shade under a clump of palms, and took my trunks and towel out of the boot. I walked a few hundred yards along the blistering pavement, found a deli where I could buy beer, sandwiches and a newspaper, then hurried down to the beach.

Predictably, the area between the flags was crowded, but the long stretch of hummocky sand in front of Virginia's bungalow was practically deserted. I headed for the wide-open spaces, looking for a convenient observation-post.

The sand felt even hotter than the pavement. As soon as I had found a suitable place to settle, I buried the beer, changed into my trunks, and spread my shirt out to dry. The sun scoured my bare skin like glass-paper. I was well-tanned, but I wasn't going to be able to stand that blow-torch heat for long. I skimmed quickly through the paper. There was no mention of Johnny Parvo, but Archer's suicide was still getting a lot of space. It was obvious that the editor suspected that there was something fishy about it, and was mad as hell because he didn't know what it was. There were dark hints about 'cover-ups' and 'the integrity of public servants'. The inquest had been postponed, presumably, so the article suggested, to give the police more time to apply the whitewash.

Still nothing moved at the bungalow. Nobody called, nobody came out. The curtains stayed drawn across the windows.

The sun inched higher, and with every passing minute, the cool blue of the ocean looked more inviting. The surf curled in lazily, each wave a bold, sweeping, mile-long swath of foam; and its thunder boomed along the shore like the sound of distant battles.

I ambled down to the water's edge, and waded in. The coolness was like a blessing. I stood and let the waves hit me, the big ones rocking me almost off my feet. There was a fierce undertow, but I felt safe enough, since I was well within my depth. Best of all, I still had a clear view of the white bungalow; now I could keep watch without being fried alive.

'Excuse me sir!' A young man in floppy trunks and a tight, wrinkled bathing-cap regarded me reproachfully from the beach. I didn't recognize him at first; my attention was fully occupied with his magnificent physique. He was a tower of a man, and his shoulders and chest seemed to be sculpted from massive slabs of muscle. He shaded his eyes with his hand; as he moved his arm, the biceps bulged like overfed pythons. Tufts of yellow hair showed under his cap, at the nape of the neck, and his nose was liberally smeared with zinc ointment. 'I'm afraid bathing is only permitted between the flags.'

I recognized the voice. 'Hello again,' I said.

'Uh—beg pardon, sir?'

'We've met before. In the car-park of the Starbird Motel.'

'Oh, yeah.' He grinned. 'You were being mugged at the time. Did they catch those two guys?'

'Not yet. I see you got yourself a job.'

'Sort of. I'm still looking for something that pays, though.'

I waded towards him and he smiled, relieved that I was being sensible. 'We just can't patrol the whole beach,' he said. 'And the tides can be treacherous. Another complication is, that some of the new immigrants can't read the notices.'

'I can read,' I said. 'I just didn't look. Sorry.'

'No sweat. It's all in the—'

I had drawn level with him. His expression changed abruptly. He seized my left arm, and fell over backwards, pulling me on top of him. As I went over, his feet exploded in the pit of my stomach and propelled me bodily over his head. I landed flat on my back in the sand, winded, and feeling as if my arm had been torn out of its socket. I rolled sideways, gasping for air. His feet scuffed sand into

107

my face; I was momentarily blinded and helpless. My luck had run out at last. I wanted to shout for help, but I could only manage a hoarse croak. Instinct kept me on the move, but I knew it was hopeless: with his speed and strength he could break my neck as easily as snapping a twig.

Amazingly, his hands were gentle : helping me up, brushing the sand off my back. 'I'm so sorry, are you all right? I couldn't think of anything else to do, on the spur of the moment.' The young man's face was contorted in an expression of concern that was almost comical. 'I only just saw it in time. You were about to tread on it. Look!'

He pointed to something just above the water-line. It looked like a small jellyfish, less than three inches across. 'Watch it a moment, will you? But don't touch it!' He bounded over to the crowded part of the beach with all the exuberance of a Labrador puppy, and raced back with a small metal can 'Want to take him alive if we can,' he explained. 'The Uni Lab wants as many as possible for research.'

'What is it?'

'He looked at me wonderingly. 'Don't you know? Deadliest killer in these waters. Worse than any shark. Blue-ringed octopus. Sting is poisonous. Kills in four minutes. No known antidote.' He scooped the little creature into a can, and splashed sea water on top of it. 'Doesn't look much like a killer, does he?'

It certainly wasn't impressive. An amorphous blob, not bigger than my thumbnail, surrounded by thin, spidery tentacles. I studied it with more than a passing interest.

The young man galloped up to the beach road, the sand squeaking under the soles of his feet. I dried myself thoughtfully, and put on my shirt. My stomach was bruised and very sore; I didn't feel hungry at all. I was just digging up the beer, when the young man returned. 'You all right?' he asked.

'I'm fine,' I lied. 'Thank you for saving my life.'

He blushed from the rim of his wrinkled bathing-cap to the layer of muscle below his collar-bone. 'I just reacted on the spur of the moment,' he mumbled.

'Have a beer? It seems the least I can offer.'

'No thanks, I don't drink much. It slows my reactions.'

'You wouldn't want that,' I agreed gravely. 'I owe a lot to your motor-reflexes.' I uncapped a beer, and faced up bravely to the consequences. 'Student?'

He nodded. 'Teacher-training. Physical culture and economics.'

'Unusual combination.'

'Is it? They're what I'm interested in. My name's Ken Walters, by the way.'

'John Tallis.' We shook hands, and he sat companionably by me, watching the kids playing by the water's edge.

I said, 'I seem to have lost my appetite. Would you care for a sandwich?'

'Yes!' he said instantly. 'Yes, I would. I really would care for a sandwich. Thank you.'

I handed him the packet, and he began to eat, chewing rapidly and deliberately. He applied himself to the task as if he was determined to extract the maximum benefit from the exercise. For the sake of conversation, I said, 'You're not a Sydney-sider, are you?'

'No, I'm a country boy. North Queenslander. How did you guess?'

'Your accent. I couldn't place it.'

'Ah.'

Conversation lapsed after that for a few minutes. Then he said in tones of genuine regret, 'There only seems to be one sandwich left?'

'Be my guest.' I finished one beer and started another. To hell with my motor-reflexes, I thought.

'You're an American, aren't you?' His mind had returned to the subject of accents.

'Only half. The other half is English.'

'Why are you watching that white house?'

'What!' I gaped at him over my beer.

'You keep glancing over there. And you were staring at it when I first came up to you. You a cop or something?'

'No.'

'You look kind of edgy. Nervous. And that was a pretty rough hassle you got into yesterday. Couldn't help being curious. None of my business, of course.'

It was meant to be friendly, but for some reason it grated on my nerves. 'It's nothing sensational,' I said shortly. 'I'm just waiting for a friend.'

'Ah.' He was unabashed. 'Lives over there, does she?'

'Yes.'

'Oh.' He shrugged. 'So much for that, then.'

'What?'

'Just an idea. It came to me while I was eating your sandwiches. You look like a man who could use some help. And I'm still looking for a job.'

I laughed. 'You want to sign on as a mercenary?'

'Why not? It's no worse than some of the things I've been offered.'

'But what if it was something dishonest?'

'Then I wouldn't do it.' Typically simple and direct.

I was tempted. I could use an ally, particularly someone as competent and fearless as this young giant. But I put the thought aside. I couldn't ask him to risk his neck in my quarrel, and furthermore, he might not rate what I was doing as particularly honest. I shook my head. 'Sorry. It's not a crusade, just a little personal problem.'

'Okay then. I hope it works out for you. Thanks for the grub. See you around, I expect.' He loped away and disappeared into the mass of people in the bathing-area. As soon as he had gone, I began to feel hungry.

It was a long, hot, profitless day. The bungalow remained quiet as a grave. When the sun had lost some of its sting, I fetched more sandwiches and ate them myself. My stomach rumbled in appreciation.

I began to suspect that Virginia had been tipped off—

probably by the two queens from the Sloppy Dog Club. I cursed myself for not following up the lead last night. If she had bolted, it was going to be damnably hard to find her.

But find her I must. Now that the link was established between Helen and Virginia, it was impossible to believe that Virginia had been at the scene of the murder by accident. Had she come to warn Helen, or to point her out for the killer? Either way, it suggested that she knew the gunman's identity. I had to get the truth out of her somehow. The thought that I might be keeping vigil outside an empty burrow needled me, but no better alternative came to mind. The shadows lengthened, and a faint breeze whispered in from the sea. The crowds began to drift away from the beach. With all the people gone, I was going to be very conspicuous. I went back to the car. From there, I still had a clear but oblique view of the front of the bungalow. I went on watching, with a sullen obstinacy that masked my growing sense of frustration.

The beach was deserted, and the daylight almost gone, when it happened. A curtain moved, in the window nearest to me. Not much: a thin triangle of black gradually showed itself, and as slowly disappeared. Someone was looking out, and being extremely cautious about it.

I watched for another fifteen minutes, until it was fully dark. There was no further sign of movement. I reversed the car as far as the first side-street, and drove half-way around the block.

There was an unmade track at the back of the houses, with a row of wooden garages facing a straggling line of fences and half-grown hedges. I left the car at the end of the track, and moved quickly to the rear of the white bungalow. Many of the other houses were showing lights; laughter and pop music spilled out of an open window nearby. Virginia's house stayed dark and silent. I could see no-one about. I ducked into the garden and went to ground between two lemon trees near the back door. I

111

inched along the flower bed to the corner of the bungalow, in the cover of a thick clump of shrubbery. From here, I could see the front gate, as well as the back door. Now that I knew Virginia was inside, I had recovered my patience. I could wait her out.

In fact, I didn't have to wait long. The back door opened a crack, so quietly and slowly that the movement was barely detectable. After a long pause, it opened further, and a girl came out, carrying a canvas hold-all. She was blonde, and wore dark glasses.

I stepped out of the darkness. 'Hello, Virginia.'

She screamed and dodged back inside. I reached the door before she could close it, and heaved my weight against it. She cannoned backwards against the far wall. 'Don't shoot! For God's sake, don't shoot!' Her voice was shrill with panic. 'I don't know anything, I didn't see anything, I swear! I just—'

'Calm down, Virginia,' I said. 'I won't hurt you. I just want to talk to you.'

'Virginia?' The voice dropped to a whisper. 'Who the hell are you?'

'I'm the fellow you've been hiding from all day. Let's get some light on here. There's no point in skulking in the dark any more.'

'Don't!' But she was too late. I found the switch and pressed it.

It was a bitter anti-climax to a long day. This girl was not Virginia Crewe.

We faced each other in the hygenically white kitchen for a long moment without speaking. Some of the fear seemed to leave her, and her shoulders slumped in resignation. She repeated, in a curiously flat, childish voice, 'Please don't shoot me!' But it was a mechanical reaction. Her mind was elsewhere.

She was blonde, like Viriginia, but there the resemblance ended. This girl was taller and thinner. Her hair was cropped short and square, in a deliberately graceless fashion. In spite of the heat, she wore a shapeless yellow cardigan, and a pleated skirt that covered her knees. She held her head sideways, as if by habit; and a moment later, I saw the reason. A broad strawberry-mark ran shockingly down the right side of her face, in a jagged V from her hair-line to the corner of her mouth. Her wrap-around glasses had fallen off; before she clapped them on again I saw that her right eye-socket was a wrinkled mess of shiny scar tissue.

I said, as reassuringly as I could, 'I'm sorry if I scared you. I won't do you any harm. I'm looking for Virginia Crewe. This is her house, isn't it?'

'Yes.' Her face began to twitch uncontrollably.

'Is she here?'

She giggled. 'Yes.'

'Will you tell her I must talk to her?'

Her manner changed abruptly. She became off-hand and languid, like an unenthusiastic hostess. 'Would you care for a drink?'

The change of pace caught me off-balance. Before I could reply, she went on, 'I don't know you, do I? I'm Diana.'

'My name's John Tallis.'

'Hello, John Tallis. I'm Ginny's sister.' Her mouth twisted wryly. 'Ginny's ugly sister. Look at me, John Tallis. Don't you think I'm ugly?'

She backed into the far corner of the kitchen, and clawed with both hands at the fabric of her skirt, drawing the hem above her knee. Her voice whined: 'Remember what Mummy says. Look, but don't touch.' She pressed her body against the wall, arched her back, and pulled her skirt high above her hips. A low, keening sound came from deep in her throat, and she rolled her head wildly from side to side.

I was at a loss. I hadn't visualized anything like this. Virginia's crazy sister was the last thing I needed, right

113

then. Diana's movement slowed gradually, like a clockwork toy, and finally stopped. Demurely, she lowered her skirt. 'What do you think?'

'I think,' I said gravely, 'that you have magnificent legs.' Might as well speak the truth wherever possible.

She smiled. 'Thank you, kind sir.'

Her switch to normality brought a chill premonition of danger. Fear pressed its icy finger between my shoulder-blades. 'May I talk to Virginia now?'

'No.' She sighed. 'You had better come with me.'

She led the way through the dining-room into a hallway. 'In here.' She opened a door, and stood aside politely for me to enter. It was a long, high-ceilinged room, panelled in light wood. There was an elaborate hi-fi system, and shelves stacked with records. A bigger-than-life-size poster of Nureyev dominated one wall. There were armchairs in white leather, and a massive, bulging sofa. There was a girl on the sofa. She had violet eyes, a deep smooth tan, and platinum-blonde hair. She wore a long-sleeved negligée with little silver-grey feathers at the neck and wrists. She had been dead for some time. There were five small bullet holes in her left breast.

Chapter Thirteen

It was a thoroughly professional job, so the gun wouldn't be far away. I found it behind one of the armchairs: a .22 automatic with the front sight filed off. I left it on the floor. 'Who did it, Diana?'

She shook her head violently. 'I don't know! I didn't see him. I was hiding. There's a loft—you can get into it from the kitchen.'

'Why were you hiding?'

'I thought it was Them.' The fear in her voice added the capital letter. 'I thought They'd come to take me back. I couldn't bear that. Ginny understood. She knew that I couldn't bear to go back there.'

'Where?'

'The Home.' She spoke as if it was the most famous place in the world. Everybody must know where the Home was. I didn't pursue the question. 'When did it happen?'

'In the middle of the night. The phone rang and woke us up. Then somebody banged on the door, and Ginny made me hide. She let him in, and they talked for a while. They went from room to room, as if she was showing him round. Then I heard this sound, like twigs snapping. Then silence for a long, long time.'

'Did you hear what they were talking about?'

'No, just the rumble of their voices. But I could tell one was a man's voice.'

'All right. What did you do then?'

'I stayed up there and waited for Ginny to call me. I

was scared to come down in case it was a trap. I waited and waited. It was terribly hot, and there were crawling things. The house was terribly quiet. In the end, I had to come down, and I found her. I guess I must have passed out then; I don't remember the next bit too well. All I could think of, was that I couldn't be here alone after it got dark.'

'Why didn't you call the police?'

'I couldn't do that! They'd send me. . . . Besides, the phone's out of order.'

'Well, we have to tell the police now, Diana.'

'No! I can't! I can't go back to that place. I'd sooner die!' She was shaking with hysteria. 'Look, if you make me go to the police, I'll tell them you shot my sister!'

'What!'

'I will, I swear I will! How do I know you didn't do it, anyway? I'll tell them I saw you do it. They'll believe me.'

They probably would. I'd been sitting outside the bungalow all day; I'd even talked to the Walters boy about it. My fingerprints would be on the back door, and probably half-a-dozen other places. If the cops caught me on this one, on top of everything else, they'd lock me away and grill me till I curled up at the edges.

'Diana,' I said desperately, 'please try to understand. Your sister was killed because of something she knew. If the killer suspects that she passed on the information to you, he may try to silence you, too. You're in great danger. You must tell the police the truth.'

'Oh, the truth! I told you, I don't know who he was; I didn't see him. I won't go to the police! What good would it do? Anyway—' She hung her head and scuffed her shoes in the carpet. 'I do know what Ginny was killed for.'

My voice emerged as a strangled shout. 'What do you mean?'

'Get me away from here, and I'll tell you.' The set of her mouth looked smug. 'Take me somewhere safe, and promise not to hand me over to . . . anyone, and I'll show you a

116

secret.'

I didn't know whether to believe her or not, but I daren't waste time thinking about it. Even if this latest gambit was just a figment of her disordered imagination, I had to go along with it. I didn't see how it could possibly make matters worse than they already were.

'Okay,' I said. 'Let's go.'

She grabbed my arm. 'Where to?'

'To see a friend.'

'Not the police?'

'Definitely not.'

She reached up and touched my cheek. 'I trust you, John Tallis.'

I made my way back to the kitchen, rubbing with my handkerchief at the surfaces I might have touched. Diana seemed amused. 'Why don't you burn the place down?'

'That would be silly and dangerous.'

'But it would get rid of the fingerprints.'

I realized she was in earnest. To her, it was a simple, practical solution to the problem. I pushed her ahead of me into the garden, and locked the back door behind us. We reached the car unobserved, as far as I could tell.

Diana liked the Lotus. She leaned back in the passenger seat, stretched her legs and purred. 'Nice. . . . If only you could spend your whole life in a motor-car, always on the move, with the world just drifting by the windows, you could feel . . . safe. At last.' She began to hum softly.

'Diana, what did you mean about showing me a secret?'

'Later,' she said dreamily. 'At your friend's place. When I'm sure you won't cheat me.'

'I won't cheat you, Diana.'

'No? Do you mind if I turn on your radio?'

She found a commercial station and hummed along with the pop records for a while. In amongst the music and the frenzied inane chatter, there was one news bulletin of interest: Johnny Parvo's car had been recovered from the sea. The report said that small particles of yellow paint,

117

probably from another vehicle, were found adhering to the car's rear fender; and the police attached great importance to this clue.

I'll bet they did, I thought. Bullock had already commented on the damage to the Lotus: he wouldn't be slow to see the significance of the new evidence. I glanced at Diana, but I could read no expression behind those dark glasses. She had hoisted up her skirt again, and seemed to be admiring her splendid legs. They were worth admiring. I wondered if their shapeliness compensated her for the disfigurement of her face. An obscure and impersonal shiver of lust trickled over my nerve endings. I opened the window a little wider.

The air that rushed in was cool and scented with eucalyptus. It should have been a pleasant drive, but I was too pre-occupied to enjoy it. As far as I could assess the situation, I was fleeing from an unreported crime with a mentally unbalanced child, in a car that the police were almost certainly looking for.

Surprisingly, we reached Double Bay without incident, and I parked the car in a side-street some distance away from Mick's house. As I made to get out, Diana said, 'You've left the keys in the ignition.' For a nut-case, she was sharply observant at times.

'A lot of people, including the police and a ruthlesss killer, are going to be looking for this car,' I said. 'If anyone is fool enough to pinch it, good luck to him.'

'That's just silly.' She reached for the keys and put them in her handbag. 'You don't know when you might need your car in a hurry.'

I shrugged. The Lotus was now far too conspicuous to be safe, but it would be a waste of time trying to explain. My immediate concern was to get this lunatic creature off my back. I didn't hope for much from her promised information. I doubted whether her mind could make any clear distinction between the real and the imaginary. On the other hand, she was my only close link with Virginia, who had obviously known something. Too much for her own good.

Mick's house was in darkness, and there was no response to the doorbell. As we waited on the porch, the phone inside the house began to ring.

'What shall we do now?' whispered Diana. 'Wait?'

'I guess so.'

The phone went on ringing. Someone was determined to get an answer.

'Let's try the garage,' I said.

Mick was not the most careful of householders. His garage doors were unlocked, and his white AC convertible was inside, with the keys in the ignition. Diana whistled, and ran her fingers along the bonnet. 'I've never seen one of these before. I bet it moves.'

'It does,' I agreed. It was odd that Mick had left it behind. He couldn't have gone far.

'Are we going to wait here?' Diana asked.

'May as well.'

She wandered around, looking at the jumble of things on the shelves and the workbench. 'Where does this door lead to?'

'The house. It's an integral garage.'

'Oh.' She examined the door closely. 'It doesn't look very strong.' She wandered back. 'That phone bothers me.'

It bothered me too. It had been ringing for an unnaturally long time. I went back to the garage doors, to keep a lookout for Mick.

There was a sharp, splintering crack behind me. I spun round, my nerves jumping. 'What the hell—?'

Diana stood by the open door, holding a tyre-lever. 'I've just done your friend a favour. That door was altogether too flimsy. Lucky for him we're not criminals.' She pushed through the shattered door and passed into the house as composed as a Sunday-school teacher. 'I'd rather wait indoors,' she explained. 'It's more comfortable. And I have to pee.'

119

The phone had been silent for a couple of minutes. It began to ring again as soon as we were inside. I picked it up. A woman's voice, momentarily startled, said 'Oh! Is that Mr Dooley's residence?'

'Yes.'

'Are you a relative of Mr Dooley?'

'As far as I know,' I said, 'his relatives are all in Ireland. I'm just a friend. What's happened? Is anything wrong?'

'Mr Dooley has been admitted to St Ann's Hospital following an accident,' she said crisply. 'We are trying to contact his family.'

My throat felt dry. 'What sort of an accident? Is he seriously hurt?'

'He is suffering from concussion. The cause of the injury has not yet been determined. The police have been informed, as a matter of routine.'

'Can I see him?'

'I don't know what that would achieve. He is unconscious at the moment. I would suggest that you phone us in the morning.' She rang off.

Diana came out of the bathroom. She had cleaned herself up a little, and the strawberry-mark glowed darkly against the pallor of her face. 'Bad news?'

I nodded. 'My friend's been hurt in an accident.'

'The one who owns this house?'

'Yes.'

'So I'm safe here for a while?' She had an infallible instinct for her own self-interest. Even her sister's death seemed to have left her untouched; it was effortlessly forgotten, like some unlikely episode of a T.V. soap-opera.

'Safe enough.' The long day in the sun had sapped my energy; I needed to relax, preferably with a long, cool drink. 'Now, what's all this about a secret?'

'Oh, that.' She was bored. 'Ginny gave me these to keep for her, just before she got killed. Here.'

'She rummaged in her handbag and produced two photographs and a cassette of recording tape.

For a change, the photographs weren't pornographic. One was of a plump, dark-haired woman, about twenty years old, at a guess. She was lying on her back, with her head turned sideways, staring at the camera. She wore a frilly housecoat, short enough to show her knees. I had never seen her before.

The other photograph was of a furniture van.

The tape-cassette gave no answers, just a whole new set of questions. I played it on Mick's machine, and listened to minute after minute of silence. The tape-hiss went on and on, and my straining ear filled its whisper with a thousand ghost voices. I turned up the volume. The scream, when it came, nearly blasted me out of the room.

I readjusted the controls, wound back the tape, and listened again. It was a harsh, high-pitched scream, followed by a dry retching. Then a thump, like a mallet on wood. Then more silence.

Finally, a voice: 'Now why in hell's name did you have to do that? She's dead.'

That was all. I played the tape to the end, reversed it and played the other side. Nothing.

Diana appeared in the doorway. She had appropriated Mick's bathrobe, which hung on her like a gaudy tent. She still wore her dark glasses. 'I heard a scream?'

'On this thing. Have you heard this tape before?'

'No.'

'Have you any idea why these photographs should be important?'

She yawned. 'No. I'm going to have a drink, and then I'm going to bed.'

She found the drinks cupboard, and poured Scotch for us both. I tried one more question: 'What did Virginia say, when she gave you these things?'

'I don't remember. She just handed them up to me. I think she said, "Hang on to these till I get rid of this joker",' or something like that. But she wouldn't have done that if they weren't important.'

The drink was making me sleepy. I had the tantalizing feeling that all the pieces of the puzzle were now in my hands, if only I could interpret them. Something was staring me in the face, waiting to be recognized. My mind was stuttering like a slipping clutch, too tired to function properly. Some of the whisky slopped on to my trousers. I put the glass down, closed my eyes, and brought all my concentration to bear on the problem.

Someone took my shoes off. I had no idea how long I had been asleep, but it wasn't long enough. My eyes seemed to have crusted over, like old port. Diana's voice was calm and soothing: 'I've been keeping watch. There's not a soul about. We're safe here.' I couldn't attach any meaning to the words, but the tone was reassuring. I nodded in dumb gratitude, and went back to sleep.

When I woke, the first glimmer of dawn was showing at the edges of the curtains. I was in bed, naked, half-covered by a cotton sheet; but I had no recollection of how I got there. Diana lay with her back to me, breathing deeply and evenly, apparently asleep. I could just make out the curve of her shoulder against the light. In spite of the pressing heat, I was chilled by a premonition of impending disaster. There was no obvious reason for my unease, but as the minutes slipped by, I couldn't rid myself of the feeling that something appalling was about to happen. I was suddenly more afraid than I have ever been; and the fear was the worse for being causeless.

Diana turned her head cautiously: she was not sleeping after all. I lay quite still and watched her. Apparently satisfied, she sat up and slowly swung her feet to the floor. She stood for a moment, listening. She was quite naked. Her silhouette was beautiful: slim and straight, with firm, round breasts and sweetly-curving hips. Her profile, seen for the first time without the distraction of her deformity or her glasses, was dramatically fine, with strong, clean lines from brow to chin. She was a two-dimensional study in black: even her shining blonde hair was a tousled black

122

cap. . . .

The catastrophe that had been building up inexorably from the minute I woke in that strange bed, now struck with the force of a thunderbolt. I began to tremble, and there was a dreadful constriction in my throat. An unbearable pain spread sickeningly downwards from my chest. I tried to speak, but my tongue clicked uselessly in my mouth.

The dark shape moved; its head swivelled towards me. Invisible eyes in a black, featureless face. But I had already recognized the profile: I knew it better than my own. . . .

It was Helen.

Chapter Fourteen

I scrambled out of bed and switched on the light. Diana regarded me calmly. 'So you finally guessed,' she said. 'I began to think I was going to get away with it. What a pity.' She scooped up her canvas holdall and took a gun out of it: a .22 automatic with the front sight filed off.

But for once I was ahead of her. I chopped the gun to the floor, and in a reflex action of explosive fury, back-handed her across the room. She slammed against the wall, and her knees began to buckle. I dragged her into the bathroom, and rubbed at the strawberry-mark on her face with a flannel. The paint came away in blotches, seeping redly into the damp cloth. The shrivelled eye-socket was made of rubber latex. It peeled off complete with its web of transparent scar-tissue. I yanked out a tuft of her hair. It had been bleached very recently, but the line of black at the roots was clearly visible.

Diana dried her face and looked at me quizzically. 'So now you know.' She smiled, a familiar-seeming smile that turned my heart over 'Now what!'

I still couldn't believe it. Stripped of its disguise, this was Helen's face, down to the smallest detail. Not even the blonde hair made any essential difference: if it hadn't been for the dark glasses and the scars, I would have seen the resemblance at once. But then, Diana had put up an effective smoke-screen of other distractions.

'Who are you?' My own voice seemed strange to me.

'Does it matter? I've sort of got used to Diana. Why

124

not stick to that?'

'Not Heidi?'

'Call me Heidi if you like. The paying customers did. It's no more real than the other name.'

'Get your clothes on,' I said tightly. 'You've got a lot of talking to do. The truth for a change.'

'The truth?' She mocked me. 'We don't need clothes for that. What better truth is there than this?' She slid her arms around me and pressed her body against mine. 'This is the truth, Mister; no pretence about this. I've been going mad for you all night. And I know you want me. I can see it in your face.'

I pushed her away and slapped her again. 'You stupid bitch, do you think I don't know that Helen was killed because of you?'

She bit her lower lip. 'You enjoyed doing that, didn't you John? And you know that I liked it too. Why don't you really let yourself go? Baby, that would be really wild. Don't run away from yourself, John. Don't be afraid. I'm not.'

Wordlessly, I thrust her back into the bedroom, and pointed to her clothes. She shrugged herself into Mick's bathrobe again, and dropped sullenly into a chair. 'I need a cigarette.'

I found a pack in her handbag and threw them over to her. I collected my own clothes and dressed quickly. Diana studied me with a cool appraisal, as if it was a performance I was putting on for her benefit.

I checked the gun. There were three rounds in the clip and one in the breech. I put the clip in my pocket and pointed the gun at Diana. 'Now.'

She looked from the gun to my face and back again. 'You're a fool. I know you won't use that thing.'

I squeezed the trigger and the little gun cracked once. It really did sound like a branch snapping. I caught the empty shell as it was ejected, and put it carefully away. A chip of plaster flew past her ear; she twisted her head

125

to look at the bullet-gouge in the wall. It was at least a foot away from her head, but it probably seemed less, where she was sitting. Some of the complacency left her face. 'Your life isn't all that important to me, Diana. I know most of the answers anyway.' I took the clip out of my pocket and slammed it back into the butt. 'There are three bullets left in here. I shan't waste another one. Now, I suggest that you pick up the story from the time when you were calling yourself Mrs Heidi Saxon, and lived in an apartment at 15a Frank Street, with another whore who called herself Dawn.'

That rattled her. 'You know about that?'

'I know a lot of things. I know about the porno pictures, and the blackmail. I know that Helen Simons was murdered because of her fantastic resemblance to you. I know that she was killed by a man they call the Dancer, who works for a protection mobster named Rick Lucy. I know that Lucy's mob is still trigger-happy about something, and I can guess what it is. But I don't need to guess any more. You're going to fill in the gaps for me.'

'You're wrong.' Her mouth tightened.

'I don't think so, Mrs Saxon. Start talking.'

She shook her head.

I said, 'I'll give you a slow count of three to change your mind. Then I'll pull the trigger.' I rested the barrel of the .22 against the bridge of her nose. 'One.'

She smiled scornfully.

'I told you, I don't need you alive,' I pointed out. 'I can find out the rest without you. You're just a short-cut. Two.'

Her face was gaunt with tension. She tried to keep the smile in place, and fixed her eyes on mine, determined to call my bluff.

'Three.'

She let out her breath in relief. She had won.

I squeezed the trigger.

The hammer clicked on the empty shell I had slipped

into the top of the clip. The ejector spat the metal case onto the floor.

'Misfire,' I said flatly. 'You were lucky. Let's start again. One.'

But she couldn't face it again. 'You bastard!'

'Two.'

'All right, all right! I'll tell you. But stop crowding me.' She lit another cigarette and started talking. 'Virginia was the one who started it all, and kept it going. At first, it was just for the money, but later it was something else: she got hooked on the excitement, the danger, the sheer devilment of it all. I met her about two years ago. She lent me money, found the flat in Frank Street for me. I was down and out then: dead broke and new to the game. The other girl—Dawn—was in Ginny's debt, too. Dawn had the ground-floor flat, number 15, I had 15a, which was the first floor, and the landlord had 15b, the top floor.'

'The landlord—he was a newspaper reporter?'

'You might call him that, if you were feeling generous. He's done some free-lance stuff. He's a photographer. Name of Julius Speichel.'

'Where can I find him?'

She shook her head. 'Wait. You want the whole story, you'll have to take it as it comes. Jules knew what Dawn and I did for a living, of course, and fixed the rent accordingly. He also expected to sample the goodies for free. He's a creep. Well, pretty soon, he's asking us to pose for sex photos in lieu of the rent, see? So, okay. But right away we run into a snag. The only male models we could hire were strictly from Crumbsville. They wanted to *act* everything, for God's sake! Nine times out of ten, the end product was not just lousy, it was laughable. So then Ginny had this idea. Why not install a two-way mirror in my bedroom? That way, Jules could get some very interesting action shots. I didn't dig the idea a whole lot, but the others got excited over it, and I have to admit, I was curious. Well, I won't go into details, but it was a hell of a lot

127

harder to set up than it sounds. To make it worse, Jules got more and more elaborate. As well as the two-way mirror, he fixed a wide-angle lens in the ceiling, and wired the place for sound, so that he had a whole movie-studio set-up, candid camera style. Finally it was ready, and Dawn and I took turns with the mugs while Jules and Virginia ran the cameras and recording equipment. Man, it was a disaster. A floperoo. After all that expense, we didn't get a single picture we could use. None of the photos was sexy. Not at all. Funny, yes. Pathetic, yes. Sexy? No, sir. I thought we'd scrap the whole thing, but Jules and Ginny were determined to go on. I couldn't figure it out at first, but it made sense later.'

'Blackmail?'

'Virginia had been aiming at that all along. The profits were bigger than porn, and the effort a lot less. You'll think I'm stupid, but I didn't see what was going on till the bust-up came.'

'So you didn't know that Merv Archer was being black-mailed, for instance?'

'Let me tell it my way. Everything is joined to every-thing else. Merv Archer was trying to get evidence against the protection gang. Naturally, Dawn and I were paying our dues to Rick Lucy, like everybody else. Merv didn't get the gen he wanted, but he got something else. Me. We needed each other from the first moment. And when we made it together, it was like nothing else in the world.'

'I saw the pictures,' I commented drily. 'I don't need to read the book.'

'You squares are all the same. If it's not your scene, you label it poison. Merv and I had fun.'

'Yes. Five thousand dollars' worth.'

'That much?' She looked haggard. 'I never knew that. I didn't even know till later, that they'd filmed us. Well sir, now we move on to the big one. The crunch. The night that changed everything. As usual, it sprang out of an idea of Ginny's. You see, Dawn and I paid fifty dollars a week to the Lucy gang. Each, that is. Then all of a sudden, he ups the rate to a hundred dollars a week. Dawn gets furious, talks about refusing to pay. But we've heard about what happens to girls who don't pay. And this is where Ginny gets her brainwave. Let's get the guys into the peephole bedroom, and film the whole extortion deal! With that kind of evidence safely stashed away, the gang daren't touch us. And we wouldn't have to fork out another cent.' Diana lit another cigarette from the stub of the previous one. 'Dawn got carried away with the idea. She not only wanted to be on the film, she wanted to embroider the scenario. Like, she would defy the thugs, get them to threaten her, before she finally handed over the money. It was a great little scene, and it ran like clockwork. Only with one small difference. When Dawn defied them, they didn't just threaten her. They killed her.'

'Who did?'

'Rick Lucy, Johnny Parvo and a man they call the Dancer.'

'Rick Lucy himself? He was there?'

'They say he often turns out to watch, if there's going to be any rough stuff. But he doesn't participate.'

'I see. And Speichel got all this on film?'

'Every last bit. Including Act two. The Dancer and Parvo drove up next morning in a furniture van. They rolled the body up in a carpet and carried it out of the house in full daylight.'

'How long ago was all this?'

'About eight or nine months. You can imagine the state we were in. Especially Jules and Virginia. This was going to be the biggest score of their lives. I went along with it because they were the only friends I had. And frankly, the murder had scared me out of my wits. We quit the Frank Street house fast, taking only the camera equipment and personal belongings with us—we had to leave the furniture behind. As soon as we were safely under cover, Jules put the bite on Rick Lucy.'

I picked up the photograph and the spool of tape. 'This was the come-on in the blackmail threat?'

'Right. That's Dawn's body, and that's the furniture van they used. The tape is part of the sound-track of the film. Lucy knew what they meant, all right. He paid fifty thousand dollars for the whole film.'

'Did he get it?'

'He got one complete print. Five months later, he got a demand for a quarter of a million dollars.'

'That's pretty greedy.'

'They changed their ideas. At first, they'd planned to leech onto Lucy's operation for a percentage of the weekly take. On second thoughts, that seemed too dangerous, so they went for the big pot. After that, we were going to split before the gang caught up with us. Which they were always liable to do, because the whole scenario had one big flaw.'

I nodded 'You.'

'Exactly. The strong-arm boys knew me, knew my face. I was even on those cruddy photographs, for God's sake! Rick Lucy put a price on my head. Forty thousand dollars. But would you believe, Ginny had the answer? She knew of a girl who looked so like me, she was virtually my double. Helen Simons. Virginia claimed Lucy's blood-money, and fingered the Simons girl for the killers.'

'She deliberately killed a total stranger?'

'You didn't know Virginia. That was her style. There was only room for one person in Ginny's world, and that was her own sweet self. And I said, the excitement of it all was like a drug to her. Earlier that day, I had dumped some clothes, money and stuff in Helen's flat. We wanted to convince the gang that they had got the right woman.'

'There was something else, I said. 'A wedding ring in Helen's handbag.'

'Ginny put it there, just after the killing. She ran across to help, see? Too easy.'

I shivered. It had all been too easy, too brutally casual.

130

'What went wrong after that? You obviously didn't get the money, or you wouldn't be here.'

'Ginny and I didn't get the money. I think Speichel got it, and went to ground. He's probably too scared to move. So that's it, John Tallis. Now you know it all.'

'Not quite,' I said. 'You missed out the important bits. Who the Dancer is, for instance.'

'I thought you knew. He's Rick Lucy's top hatchet-man.'

'What does he look like?'

She considered. 'Something like you, actually. Big. Has an American accent.'

That wasn't much help. I changed the subject. 'Where is Julius Speichel?'

She laughed. 'So you finally got around to it! The only thing that really matters. But the Dancer's the one you really want, isn't he? The rest of us are just walk-ons. He's the star, the main attraction: he actually pulled the trigger. Trouble is, you don't even know what he looks like. You could pass him in the street and never know it. What you do know, is that his face is on film. And Jules Speichel has that film. I'll say this for you, John Tallis, you get there in the end, though you're as subtle as an Army tank. Okay, I'll offer you a trade.'

'You've got nothing to bargain with.'

'You're wrong, as usual. I know how badly you want that information. You're like a dog that's smelt the rabbit. The quickest way to get what you want, is to trade.'

'Okay. What do you want?'

'Time. A chance to get clear. The cops don't know yet, that I'm involved. They may not even know I exist. I want you to keep it that way as long as possible: long enough to give me a head start.'

'How do we know we can trust each other?'

'I'll have to trust you. You don't have to trust me very far, since you can check out my information within an hour. I need a longer start than that. At least two days.'

'It's a deal.'

131

'Good.' She rose from the chair and wrapped herself more tightly in the bathrobe. 'But first, we're going to eat. I'm starving.'

So was I, although I hadn't realized it until the smell of cooking woke agonizing pangs of hunger in my stomach. We breakfasted off steak and eggs, washed down with pints of good coffee. Diana's appetite was as huge as mine. Afterwards, she smiled crookedly. 'Strange how one's basic needs make the most bizarre situations commonplace.'

I was startled: it was as if she had read my mind. If it hadn't been for this girl, Helen's murder would never have happened; yet here I was, sharing a meal with her as if we were the closest of friends. Diana didn't give me time to brood on it. 'Jules Speichel is short and plump, has receding hair and wears gold-rimmed spectatcles,' she said crisply. 'But the most noticeable thing about him, is that the backs of his hands are covered with thick black hair, almost like fur. His latest hide-out was a derelict bungalow in Milsom's point. I don't know if he's still there, but it's likely. The bungalow is down by the harbour, next to a run-down warehouse. It's empty because the property company that owns it is hoping to buy the warehouse and develop the whole area. They're put a big fence round the bungalow and a notice saying the site is protected by guard-dogs, but in fact nobody goes near the place.'

I took Mick's car, and headed into the midday traffic. The heat was worse than ever.

· Chapter Fifteen

The derelict bungalow was easy to find. It stood next to the warehouse on an irregular curve of unmade dirt-track that dipped steeply off the bay-side road. I parked the car higher up the hill and walked down the track. The loose dirt underfoot crunched like frozen snow-crystals, and the bone-white outline of the wooden house shimmered in the heat.

There was a steep bank on the landward side of the track, thickly covered with dog-rose and red-spider flower; and the strip of shade from the squat bulk of the warehouse made an unexpected oasis of coolness there. The little hollow was strangely, broodingly quiet, although there was a steady stream of traffic on the road almost vertically above. If I hadn't loitered a moment in the shade, I wouldn't have heard the voice at all.

It was not immediately recognizable as a voice. I might have taken it for the dry creaking of some rusty mooring-chain, except that the faint sound resolved itself into words. 'Oh, Christ!' it whispered. Then, after a few seconds, 'Oh, sweet Jesus bloody Christ!'

This was followed by an agonized wheezing, against a confused medley of other sounds, like someone pushing bottles around with a yard broom. Then recognizable words again, in a whispered shout: 'Don't anybody work 'ere, fer Gawd's sake? Where are yer, yer Commie bastards? Flamin' Ada, you'ld think we was an 'underd miles north o' the Black Stump! I'm goin' ter rot in this bloody rat-'ole, and no bugger cares . . . 'Allo! 'Allo!' The hoarse complaints creaked on, as tenuous as the rustle of dry leaves.

I looked round the corner of the building, into a small cobbled yard in front of a battered, but still serviceable wooden jetty. A few planks and a heap of rusting metal were piled against the wall; and near the water's edge was an upended sailing-dinghy, badly in need of a coat of paint. But of the voice's owner, there was no sign.

'Hello!' I called. 'Where are you?'

' 'Bout bloody time!' whispered the voice. 'I'm down 'ere— I've fell down the back of the bike shed!'

There was no sign of any bike shed. The voice must have realized that the description was hardly adequate, for it added testily, 'Under the flippin' chain!'

The chain hung from a block and pulley attached to a crane arm at the top of the side wall. Immediately under it were the big double doors and loading platform of the upper floor; and below that, at ground level, was a large wooden rostrum, about four foot high, in front of another doorway. It did look a little like a bicycle shed, in that it was open at the front and boarded-in at the sides; but it looked a hell of a lot more like another loading platform. Underneath it were the remains of what had been another set of doors. Slivers of rotten wood clung drunkenly to the metal hinges, and framed the darkness of a large jagged hole. I pushed the shattered doors apart, and peered down.

I couldn't see him at first, and while I waited for my eyes to adjust themselves to the darkness, he wheezed out a continuous thread of abuse in a thin, disembodied monotone, like the whining of a particularly tetchy ghost.

The cellar had probably been used as a cold store at one time: I could make out the bulky outline of wide, slatted shelves in the background. More recently, it seemed to have been a depository for furniture and long-abandoned junk of all kinds. Near the bottom of the loading-chute was a pile of cordage, paint-tins and tattered sailcloth;

and sprawled in the middle of this was a frail, white-haired old man. He was dressed in a singlet, denim trousers and Army boots, and he lay flat on his back, apparently unable to move. He gave off a ripe aroma of cheap red wine, pickled onions and cleaning fluid. Near his head lay a tatty fibre suitcase, gaping open and revealing a varied assortment of bottles, most of them broken.

' 'Urry up, can't yer?' the old man croaked. 'Stop sticky-beakin' an' get yer finger out. I ain't a flippin' peep-show!'

I lowered myself carefully; the chute was sound enough, but I didn't want to land on top of him. It wasn't much of a drop. When I reached the floor, my head and shoulders were level with the opening.

'Let's have a look at you.' I said. 'Have you broken anything?'

' 'Ow the 'ell do I know? I can't bloody move. Ain't that crook enough?' he hissed pathetically.

I didn't want to start lugging him around if any of his bones were broken. 'Are you in pain?'

'Course I am!'

'Where does it hurt most?'

'Every bloody where!'

I guessed he was all right. The ropes and sailcloth had cushioned his fall, and when he crashed through the doors, he was probably dead drunk and as relaxed as a rag doll. His feet were hopelessly caught up in a tangle of netting which had once held a string of glass floats, and the back of his vest was hooked on the end of a broken spar; but if he hadn't been as weak as a sick kitten, he could have freed himself easily. I dragged the netting off his feet, unhooked his vest, and helped him up. He immediately fell to his knees, and scrabbled recklessly among the broken glass in his suitcase, lifting out the bottles and holding them against the light. They were all empty, and he swore at them feebly but without surprise.

I hoisted him out of the cellar without much difficulty—he was as light as a child—and pitched his suitcase up

135

after him. In the daylight, he looked even older and frailer than ever. His skin, stretched tight over knife-edged bones, was blotched with dark brown freckles; and his shoulders stuck out of his tattered vest like knotty sticks. He sat down in the dust, with his legs stretched out in front of him, and leaned his back against a plank. 'You wouldn't have a wet on yer?' he whispered. 'Or a bit o' chutty?'

I shook my head. 'How long have you been down there?'

'I dunno. Seems like years. Shouted meself hoarse. Gawd, I gotta get a drink. Look, you prob'ly saved my life, sport. 'Ow about toppin' it out with the loan of a couple of bob?'

I dug in my pocket and found a half-dollar. 'You'ld do better to get yourself something to eat.'

'It's yer bloody money I want, not yer bloody advice. Anyway, it's only a loan.' He squinted contemptuously at the coin on his skinny palm. 'Bloody typical. Two 'undred years of progress to give us a five-bob piece that ain't even round!'

I was curious about something. 'Do you often sleep down here?'

'Sometimes, 'pecially when it's hot. Quiet, innit? An' it was snug in that bike shed, till the back fell out of it.'

'I should have thought you'ld be more comfortable in that bungalow,' I said. 'It's empty, isn't it?'

The old man grinned slyly. 'Depends what you mean,' he wheezed. 'Thinkin' of takin' a look round, are yer?' His bright, button-eyes regarded me with bird-like intelligence.

'I might.'

'Good luck to yer then. The gate ain't locked. They busted the catch.'

'Who did?'

He shrugged, and began the laborious business of getting to his feet. ''Ow would I know? Larrikins and toe-raggers, sneakin' round in the black of night. Commie bastards, more'n likely.' He started to shuffle off, and then turned back, weighing something in his mind. 'You done

136

me a favour,' he breathed. 'I might do one for you. D'yer want ter buy a wagon?'

'A car?'

'Dirt cheap.'

'Whose car is it? Yours?'

'As good as. Twenty dollars: whad'yer say?' He sucked air noisily through his teeth.

I grinned at him. 'I say I'd be a mug to fall for a con like that.'

He made a ratchety sound at the back of his throat. He was laughing. 'Yer a bigger mug than you know,' he croaked happily. 'It's a pleasure to do business wiv yer.' He moved off again.

I called after him: 'What's your name, old man?'

The cheap suitcase clinked as he turned to look back at me. 'Chuck Starr,' he said with dignity. 'They call me Lucky.'

I pushed open the gate and walked along the weed-grown path to the back of the house. The place was not badly dilapidated. A few windows were broken, and the gaps carefully boarded over. The white paint was nothing more than a thin film of dust over bare boards, but the structure itself looked sound enough.

The wooden steps of the back verandah clattered under my feet, and the warped screen-door creaked a protest as I eased it open. I waited for a couple of minutes, but I could hear no movement inside the house. I took the .22 out of my pocket, and pushed cautiously at the back door. It opened easily and smoothly on greased hinges. I stepped into a wide, shallow living-room, empty, apart from a couple of broken-backed armchairs. The smell of cigarette smoke hung in the air, stale, not recent. Other smells too, less definable, lurked in the corners: musty, decaying smells.

There was no point in being furtive: I had made too much noise already. I called out: 'Speichel! Julius

137

Speichel!' My voice was resonant in the bare room. Nobody answered and nothing moved. The echoes seemed only to emphasize the stillness.

In the kitchen, a dry whisper of movement made my nerves leap, and an army of cockroaches scurried for shelter. Someone had eaten here, but not too recently; the crumbs on the floor were rock-hard, and the unwashed pans on the Calor-gas stove were furred and mouldy. If Speichel had been here at all, it looked as if he had moved on. But perhaps I was under-estimating his subtlety; maybe he had left the kitchen in that state deliberately.

I hunted through the remaining rooms rapidly and methodically. None of them was completely empty. There were splintered packing-cases, filthy mattresses, even a wardrobe and baby's cot; but no sign of any recent occupation by anything but rats and bugs.

Until I came to the last, and largest bedroom. Someone had been living there. There were two camp beds, one of them piled high with rugs and blankets; a rickety chest of drawers; and a lot of luggage. Four suitcases, a grip and a trunk were spaced in an irregular line across the room. Two of the suitcases lay open, and clothes—male and female—were strewn everywhere. Most of the clothing had been dumped by the trunk, but the rest trailed untidily across the beds and lay in random heaps in every corner. A razor and a silver-backed brush were on the floor by the chest of drawers. The brush was engraved on the back in ornate Gothic script: J.S. So Diana had kept her part of the bargain. Julius Speichel had been here after all.

But where was he now? And who had scared him out of his bolt-hole so unexpectedly that he had left all his belongings behind?

Not quite all his belongings, I realized. There were no papers of any kind among the litter on the floor, and nothing at all in the chest of drawers. Speichel was a photographer; but there were no cameras, no film, no photo-

138

graphic equipment of any kind in view. The suitcases and the grip were all empty.

There was something about the room that made my flesh creep. In spite of the sultry heat, my hands were like ice. A fat fly zig-zigged crazily through the still air, and threw itself recklessly at the window-pane. Something nagged at my senses, clamouring for attention. Something was wrong with that room, out of place. . . .

It was the smell. A faint smell of burning, a compound of singed horse-hair and overcooked meat. That smell didn't belong in that room. There was no reason for it.

After a long moment of indecision, I looked in the only place left to look. And I found him.

He lay on his back in a crumpled white suit, strapped to the bed with thin nylon cord. His face was invisible: it had been swathed round and round with bandages, like a mummy's head, with only his mouth left uncovered. His hands, hairy as a gorilla's, lay on his chest. His feet were bare, and hideously burned. Whatever secrets Speichel had, he had told them all before he died.

The stench that rose from the body assaulted my throat and nostrils, and I reared away, gasping and retching. I was still fighting to get some clean air into my lungs when two men came quietly into the room. I had met them before. Then, they had hit me with their fists. This time, they changed their style. The big one hit me with a cosh, high up on the shoulder. It felt as if it had broken my collarbone. The younger one was gentler, more scientific. He hit me just below the ear. I sighed gently, and passed out.

Chapter Sixteen

The noise was all round me, deafening, vibrating; as stupefying as a boiler foundry in mid-shift. My head felt as if someone was hammering a spike through it. I woke painfully into a stifling darkness. A close-coffined darkness, smelling of metal and oil. The noise battered at my senses, scrambled my wits. It took me several minutes to work out where I was, and the knowledge brought me no comfort. I was wedged in the trunk of a car. I had been trussed like a chicken, and gagged with adhesive tape. I could raise my head only a couple of inches before it struck metal; I couldn't move my arms and legs at all.

Panic clawed at my belly; the horror of suffocating to death in that tin box descended on my mind like a red mist. Sweat popped out of my forehead and ran off my face in slow-crawling rivulets. A thousand speculations crowded into my head, each one nastier than the one before. Assuming that they were planning to get rid of me, how would they do it? Run the car into the harbour? Crash it somewhere, and set fire to it? I'd read that a man can survive for thirty seconds in a blazing car. My imagination dwelt picturesquely on those thirty seconds, before I could wrench it away. Whatever they had in mind for me must surely be more private than that? The thought wasn't much in the way of consolation, but I made the most of it. I lay there as inanimate as a sack of potatoes, trying to reconcile my mind to the feeling of utter helplessness. I was parched with thirst, my legs were numb,

140

and there was a spot between my shoulder-blades that felt as if it was being excavated by an ice-pick. I squirmed around, and after innumerable attempts, managed to achieve a fractional change of position.

The physical relief was out of all proportion to my actual success; and the achievement did something for my morale, too. The panic receded a little.

We were moving in fits and starts: the noise that surrounded me was the growl of city traffic. I banged my head against the roof of the trunk, hoping to attract attention, but I knew it was hopeless. I couldn't compete with the rush-hour din; all I was doing was to acquire a few more bruises. I forced myself to relax, to conserve my strength.

The trip seemed interminable. The air grew thick and foul, and great waves of dizziness drifted over me. I could no longer concentrate; my thoughts scattered and slid away like quicksilver. In spite of the cramp in my limbs, I lapsed into a drowsy stupor, and floated back into unconsciousness as gently as a leaf sliding along the surface of a stream.

The second awakening was worse than the first. I knew immediately where I was, and the predicament I was in. My whole body was racked with agonizing cramps, and the realization that I was still trapped in that metal coffin brought the first dreadful stab of claustrophobia.

We were out of the city traffic now: the engine note had changed to a steady, high-pitched whine, and the tyres thrummed deafeningly close to my head. After a long time, the car slowed down to a jolting crawl, and dirt drummed against the underside. We had left the main road. The lurching motion rattled me round like a bug in a box; I couldn't tell how many miles we covered in this fashion, but the shaking threatened to loosen every tooth in my head.

Branches scraped along the metalwork, and dry scrub crackled under the tyres. At last we lurched to a stop. When

141

the engine note died, silence settled like a sudden deafness. There was a businesslike clunking of doors, a dry scratching in the lock, and a flood of fresh air that made my senses stagger. The daylight was more than I could bear; I squeezed my eyes tight against it, and felt hot tears sting my cheeks.

Hands pulled at me urgently, rolled me out over the back fender onto rocky scrubland. Thorns pricked my hands and face; thin, dry stalks crackled under my weight like tissue-paper. The air was oppressively still, and as heavy as a cartload of wet wool. Reluctantly, I forced my eyes open.

There were four of them: Bev, Polly, and two new faces. I felt a sharp, irrational pang of disappointment: neither of the strangers could be the Dancer. They were too small. I was absurdly aggrieved that I was going to die without even seeing his face.

The elder of the two strangers took charge. He was dressed for the stage rather than the bush, in immaculate white ducks and a navy blazer with steel buttons. He had a deeply-tanned, beaky face, silver hair, and small, white teeth. 'Over there,' he said, pointing. 'Cover him up.'

Polly and Bev dragged me a few yards deeper into the bush, watched by Silver-hair and the other stranger, who was the most bizarre-looking of the lot. He wore a green baseball-cap over shoulder-length hair, and an orange tee shirt with a Mickey Mouse emblem on the chest. His flared slacks were in vertical wasp-stripes of yellow and black. He had a wispy, mandarin moustache, and gold-rimmed spectacles. He supervised the arrangement of a crude screen of branches over me. When they had finished, I couldn't see them at all, though I could hear most of the muttered conversation that followed.

Silver-hair did the talking. His voice was familiar: I had heard it before, on the cassette-tape. That made him Rick Lucy. 'Me and Bev'll take care of our hero,' he said. 'Joe, you drive back to the boat. Stay on board, and stay

142

near a phone. We won't need you unless there are any complications. Polly, you go with him. Get another car, and be at this spot—' there was a rustle of paper— 'here at exactly 1.30 a.m. Not before, understand? We ought to be there by then. If we're not, wait for us. Clear?'

There were murmurs of assent. Bev's voice cut through, sounding nervous and aggrieved. 'Why isn't the Dancer here? How come we're doing his job for him?'

'The Dancer's chasing some crazy idea of his own. He'll be choked that we beat him to the mark.'

Polly's deeper voice chimed in: 'Yeah, did we tell you about that damfool caper he pulled the other morning? Like a stage play, it was.'

'You told me. Now you and Joe better get going.'

'One moment, Rick.' This must be Joe's voice: light, pedantic. 'I want to be sure of one thing. This business ends here, doesn't it? There's nobody else to be hit?'

'Right.'

'The Dancer seems to think different.'

'The Dancer's always trying to complicate things. Look, there were three people in that Frank Street house, right? Those three people are dead. This joker's the last loose end. We always knew there had to be one other guy, from the way the caper was worked. The Dancer had some crazy idea it was a woman; I knew it had to be the guy Heidi Saxon was shacked up with. That's why we burned out his apartment. And the clincher is this—the cops found a movie camera among the burnt-out wreckage. Now Speichel was the photographer, but we didn't find any cameras at all among his stuff. See how it all fits together?'

'That corp in the bungalow—that was Speichel?'

'Right.'

'So who cooled him?'

Rick sounded amused. 'I reckon the Dancer got to him, and teased some information out of him. My guess is that the Dancer's turning the city inside-out right now, looking for the boy we got tied up in the bushes.'

143

There was a pause while they digested this. Then the precise voice asked, 'So you're gambling that the film got burned in Tallis's apartment, as well as the camera?'

'It's no gamble,' Rick said smugly. 'We got it from the horse's mouth. Look, how do you think I knew where Tallis could be picked up today?'

Joe worked it out first. 'I get it. You had a tip-off. And it had to be somebody who knew Tallis. Somebody he trusted.'

'Right. A kid who's been useful to us in the past. A neat little performer called Virginia Crewe.'

'If she's crossed Tallis, how can you be sure you can trust her?'

'Look, we can pick her up any time. And she knows it. We can trust her. Okay. Inquest's over. Time you blokes got moving.'

'Rico, there's one thing—' Bev was still puzzled. 'What's the idea, using Speichel as target practice? The guy was dead as mutton.'

'Jeeze, I nearly forgot! Glad you reminded me, son. Polly, I got another little job for you. Now, listen to this, Bev, you'll learn something. I shot Speichel with that popgun we took off Tallis, right? Now, Tallis is about to disappear. But his gun isn't. That'll be found hidden away in his motel room. And a bullet from that gun will be found in Speichel. The papers'll love it. Polly, I want you to dump the piece tonight. And to make it easy for you, here's the key to Tallis's room. If you see the Dancer, give him the glad tidings.'

Shortly afterwards, the car drove away. The engine noise faded in a long drawn-out diminuendo, so gradual that it was impossible to tell when it had finally stopped. The tiny sounds of the bush took over. Rick and Bev settled down to wait. They talked hardly at all, but from time to time they drank noisily and tossed bottles in to the bush. My own thirst was becoming a torture which hourly grew so intense that it distracted me from the squadrons of insects that were devouring me alive. The worst of the cramps had passed, but I began to notice an alarming numbness in my hands and feet.

At last, night came. The sky darkened to a powdery black, like an old man's jacket speckled with snuff. A yellow moon, swollen like an over-ripe fruit, sagged low over the stunted trees. A cluster of tiny flowers, black against the moonlight, leaned over my head, their blossoms minute beads at the end of hair-like stalks. The black beads stayed unnaturally still: there was no wind at all.

At a word from Rick, Bev cut the ropes from my legs, and heaved me to my feet. The pain of the returning circulation crippled me. I crashed down into knee-high scrub generously laced with brambles. Rick circled me warily on the uneven ground, and probed my back with his foot. 'On your feet, hero. We're going walkabout. Every time you fall down, I'll kick you till you get up. Okay?'

He kicked me enthusiastically until I got up, then shoved me in the direction I was to go. A man of his word.

Bev shone a torch on the path, but at a sharp command from Rick, doused it and put it away. They stationed themselves each side of me, and pushed me ahead of them along a barely-visible track. Rick gave me basic directions by prodding me in the ribs. The track led downhill, gradually at first; then, as the slope got steeper, the bush thickened at either side. The twisted forms of ti-trees and stunted gums crowded close around, glimmering palely in the gloom; the sparse mulga gave way to dense, tall ferns, booby-trapped with trailing brambles and straggly, long-thorned shrubs. The thick carpet of bone-dry twigs crackled underfoot like burning heather. Rick pushed on quickly, careless of the noise, confirming my suspicions that this place was as remote and uninhabited as it seemed.

Lower down, we branched off the narrow path into a wider track, littered with small boulders and slabs of dried-up clay. It was an old creek-bed, parched and waterless in the hot season; its deep furrow sliced through the bush like a railway cutting. There was hardly any vegetation underfoot here, other than spindly rushes and a few patches of soft moss; but the rocks and the loose, crumbly ground made the going much harder. I turned my ankle painfully several times; and judging from Bev's language, he was faring little better.

For a few yards, we slithered through shallow mud, and clouds of mosquitoes rose to greet us, shrilling an ecstatic welcome to the unexpected feast. They struck like a hailstorm of tiny darts, shaking the turbid air with their whining. I began to think that Rick would be spared the trouble of killing me; the mosquitoes would do the job for him.

The only grain of satisfaction in all this was that the others were suffering too. Bev's complaints had settled into a breathless string of meaningless obscenities, punctuated by convulsive slaps at his arms and neck; while Rick shook his head at the swarms like an enraged bull-terrier.

'For Chrissakes, Rico, how much further?' Bev sounded as petulant as a frustrated prima-donna.

'Shut up!' Nervous tension crackled like static in Rick's voice. As if in response to his mood, a few silky threads of cloud blurred the outline of the moon, and thunder muttered in the distance like the muffled beating of a toy drum. Not far ahead, I could see the silver glint of water through the trees. This is it, I thought dully; this is where I have to make a move, try to escape. No brilliant ideas came; my will was numbed by the effort of stumbling along that uneven track. The mosquitoes attacked with redoubled fury, their sinister wail trembling in my ears. The humid air was sticky as warm soup. I succumbed to a fatal lassitude, too weary to care any more about what would happen to me.

Without warning, Bev gave a sharp exclamation of pain, and sat down in the path. 'Hey!' he said. 'What the hell—?'

Twisted his ankle, I thought sourly. Serves him right.

146

Irrationally, I felt annoyed at this interruption in our progress. I was sick of this endless, trudging misery. The journey had gone on far too long; whatever lay at the end of it, I wanted to get there.

Rick felt the same way. 'Get up, you fool!'

Bev stayed where he was. 'Somethin' bit me,' he complained. I could hear him fumbling in his pockets, but I could see no more of him than a shadowy mass against the denser blackness of the path. It had grown much darker in the last few minutes. A cloud like a livid bruise was spreading over the lower half of the moon. Sudden light danced around us, silvering thin leaves and slabs of rock. Bev had found the torch.

Abruptly, shockingly, he screamed like a girl. He was clutching his ankle with his free hand; blood seeped through his fingers, staining his socks and trouser cuff. Already a thousand insects were treacling their wings in the sticky mess.

Bev sobbed, 'It's a tiger! Oh my God! Oh sweet Jesus!' He bounced to his feet, as if on a spring, and shone the torch wildly around. 'There! There!'

The snake was moving so fast, I saw only a blur of freckled movement and a tremor in the olive-brown foliage. I had an impression of suppleness and strength, an athlete's muscle sliding under oiled skin; I heard a sound like the dry creaking of old leather; and then nothing. Not a sound: leaves as still as if they were painted on canvas.

Bev whimpered incoherently. If he had indeed been bitten by a tiger-snake, he had some reason for panic. The tiger's venom is deadly and fast. If he could get to a hospital within the hour, and if the hospital had the right serum, Bev might have a chance. But seconds were precious.

The same thoughts had been racing through Bev's mind. The torch jittered in his hand, scattering yellow blobs of light on the motionless leaves. Beyond the circle of torchlight, the soft darkness pressed close, thickening perceptibly.

'You've got to help me!' Bev gasped. 'I'm dying!' This

last thought roused him into action. He turned and stumbled back along the path. Rick started after him shouting; he had momentarily forgotten about me. I bent double and charged at his back with my shoulder. I knocked him sprawling facedown, and scrambled up the bank for cover of the nearest patch of scrub.

I didn't attempt to get far. The bush here was as dense and spiny as a quick-set hedge. I backed into the thicket, to protect my face from the flailing branches; and when I could get no further that way, I flopped to the ground and tried to squirm between the closely-packed stems. Bev was still crashing noisily along the trail; I hoped the racket he was making had masked the sounds of my progress. I hugged the ground, scarcely daring to breathe. Unless Rick had a torch, he'd have to stumble over me to find me. It was as black as a disused mine shaft down there.

Rick took an unaccountably long time making up his mind to follow me. After a minute's thought, I worked out why. I had charged directly at the bank where the tiger-snake had disappeared.

I felt chilled, as if the sweat on my body had congealed into ice. My mind fumbled for reassuring thoughts to slow down the frantic fluttering of my heart, but without conspicuous success. I stayed scared. My skin cringed, as if the ground all around me was crawling with snakes. Perhaps it was.

Twigs crunched only yards away. Rick had started to search for me at last. I twisted my face towards the sound, but I could see nothing, not even the outlines of the undergrowth that hemmed me in. Automatically, I registered one small reprieve: Rick didn't have a torch, or he would have used it by now.

Something small and inquisitive crawled over my chin, making a business of negotiating the bristles. It tickled abominably; my skin felt as if it had been sandpapered. I concentrated my mind on trying to relax some of the tension that had petrified my neck and shoulders. My eyes were stretched open, straining into the blank darkness. The moon was obscured, and the clouds showed no sign of breaking up. Rick would have a tough job finding me as long as I stayed put and made no noise. So I had won at least a short breathing-space. I wondered what to do with it.

There was no way I could get my hands free. The rope that bound them was as tight as ever. If I daren't move, and I couldn't free my hands, I had won nothing but a few hours' reprieve. All Rick had to do, was wait. He knew I couldn't be far away.

I doubted that I could last out long, anyway. My thirst was rapidly becoming intolerable, and my imagination began to manufacture its own unsubtle tortures: ice-cold beer, mountain streams, drinking-fountains with metal cups. I even envied Chuck Starr, snug in some insanitary corner with his bottle of red biddy.

The deadwood creaked again, tentatively, as if Rick was unsure of his footing. I pressed myself into the earth, blessing the darkness. If I couldn't see him, he couldn't see me.

It was too good to last.

Lightning ran like a slow fuse across the distant horizon. For the space of perhaps a full second, the whole scene stood out in stark relief, as if lit by a flare. The ledge where I lay, thickly wooded as it was, was only about a hundred yards away from a huge expanse of water. It was not the open sea; there were hills on the other side. A lake, perhaps, or a river estuary. Immediately below me, a few yards to my right, was the black cleft of the creek bed. Rick was on the near bank, about twenty feet away, crouching, like a man sheltering in a low doorway. I could see the revolver in his hand quite clearly.

He seemed to be looking in my direction, but I couldn't tell whether he had seen me or not. After that moment of dazzling brilliance, the darkness seemed even more absolute, but it no longer gave me any assurance of shelter.

149

The next lightning-flash could come at any second.

The muffled grumble of the thunder reached us at last; the storm centre was miles away yet, below the horizon. But on the heels of that sound, came another: a rusty creaking in the trees, that slowly increased in volume, rattling the dry leaves like castanets. The wind squalled off the face of the water with a savage, mindless fury, thrashing the bushes and flattening the thin grasses like a stampede of wild animals.

I began to move; Rick would never hear me above that racket. And by the same token, I wouldn't hear him: I couldn't be sure he wasn't coming straight for me. I wriggled deeper into the bush, putting as much distance between us as I could, before the wind abated.

I broke clear of the thicket, and was able to get to my feet, and make faster progress. The wind skirled on, louder than ever. To try to maintain some sense of direction, I kept the slope of the hill to my left, peg-legging over the very steep bits. I had reached a patch of loose scree, bare of any vegetation whatever, when the wind died as abruptly as it had sprung up. At the same time, I tripped on a jagged outcrop of rock, fell on my face, and slid unceremoniously down a fifteen-foot slope in a small avalanche of stones and dust.

Rick must have heard me. I tried to listen for him, but the thumping of my heart dwarfed every other sound. I was not under cover: the next lightning-flash could expose me like a searchlight. Hastily I rolled over, trying to push myself upright. The stones under me were small, sharp-edged.

My fingers encountered something smooth. And cold. And squat. Something familiar.

A beer bottle.

Australians discard their litter with the prodigality of a politician making election promises. They may never be able to tame all of their wild, unhospitable country, but they will doubtless achieve their unconquerable ambition to cover every inch of it with bottles and cans.

Clutching the bottle, and blessing the slovenly lout who had discarded it, I edged sideways, looking for cover and a chance to benefit from my new-found treasure. Thunder sighed windily in the distance, its noise competing with the rattle of the scree under my feet. At last I found what I was searching for: a wizened eucalyptus, with ragged branches forking sharply from the main stem low to the ground.

It was harder to break the bottle than I would have believed possible, but at last the glass gave way with a report like a muffled explosion. I knew the noise I was making must be leading Rick in my direction like a homing signal, but it couldn't be helped. Among the debris was a thick shard of glass with an edge like a razor; I wedged it into the fork of the tree, and began to work the nylon cord against it. The strands leapt apart so quickly that I only narrowly avoided gouging a great slice out of my wrist. My hands immediately woke from their semi-numbness to a throbbing agony.

But I was free! I felt a savage exhilaration that made my head swim. I crouched low to the ground, listening hard and massaging my swollen hands. The temperature was dropping perceptibly, minute by minute. The wind sprang up again, rustling through the dry leaves, but with nothing like its former violence.

If Rick was on the move, I couldn't hear him. My night-vision had improved to the extent that I could now distinguish the tree-tops against the sky, but that was all. The only thing that I could rely on to give me my bearings, was the slope of the ground. I tried to visualize the terrain in my mind. Downhill, about a hundred yards away, was the large expanse of water I had glimpsed in the lightning-flash. Uphill somewhere, was a dirt track leading eventually to a main road. And somewhere in the surrounding darkness, was a frightened gangster with a gun. At least, if he wasn't frightened yet, he was going to be. The hunter was about to be hunted.

But before I could formulate any plans, the breeze brought a faint, inexplicable perfume that sent a prickle of alarm along my spine. I didn't want to believe my senses. Surely Rick wouldn't be such a fool—?

A flickering light, like a single candle-flame, glinted in the undergrowth downhill to my left. It grew with incredible speed, swelling like a great golden balloon, and bursting out in every direction, scattering plump oranges of flame on the nearby branches. Within seconds, the first tinsel-spark had shaped itself into a solid pillar of flame, leaping skywards and roaring like a blowlamp. At the fringes of the blaze, the topmost leaves popped and sparkled like firecrackers. Another light appeared, to the right of the first, and then another and another. Rick was firing the bush along a line at the lower level of the hill, trusting the breeze to carry the flames up to me. He meant either to smoke me out, or burn me to a crisp.

Chapter Seventeen

It was madness. After the long drought, the woodland was as volatile as a petrol-bomb. Rick had put his own life in as much danger as mine. Surely he realized that?

My brain nagged at the problem. It was inconceivable that Rick hadn't worked out the odds on this gamble. So he must have an escape route somewhere. A boat, obviously. So he would stay by the shore, ready to shoot me down if I made a break in that direction. On the other hand, if the bush behind me was very thick, I could easily be hopelessly trapped if I tried to outrace the fire that way. It was an ugly choice, but I couldn't afford to hesitate.

The bush was silent and still no longer. Birds rocketed from the undergrowth, screaming their alarm; the ground was suddenly alive with lizards and small scurrying creatures ghostlike and two-dimensional in the flickering light. No smoke was visible above the intense white glare of the fire, but clouds of insects thickened the shimmering air.

I was on the move myself, crashing through the close-packed brushwood like a wild boar. I had to make certain assumptions. If they were the wrong ones, I was as good as dead. But I was dead for certain if I stayed where I was. I had to assume that Rick would be working towards his boat, which would therefore be to my right. I ran left, towards the first outbreak of the fire, hoping to skirt it as far away from Rick as possible.

But it soon became clear that the fire was covering the ground faster than I was. It had already spread far to the left, and was eating its way steadily uphill, narrowing and lengthening my escape corridor with every passing second. The heat was like a blast from a furnace door. As I paused, sweating, a cloud of vapour ignited with a soft whoosh about fifteen feet from the ground, and a tongue of flame snaked out like a whiplash above my head. The fumes made my eyes smart and clawed savagely at my lungs. A finger of panic played an icy arpeggio along the back of my neck. I felt trapped, hopeless. The heat was beating at me like a fist.

A few yards to my right, the foliage thinned a little, and the fire looked less intense. I folded my arms above my head and charged at the gap like a rugger forward running for the goal line. The heat was appalling. The soles of my feet were in agony after only a few yards, and the flames scourged my skin like wire whips. My clothes began to smoulder. I burst through into the dry bracken beyond the last hedge of flame, trailing sparks like a penny rocket. My breath laboured in my lungs, but I daren't stop. I pushed my aching body through the final barrier of thorn-infested bush, and emerged onto a narrow, shingly beach.

Out of the corner of my eye, I saw two orange flashes wink like semaphore signals, but I never heard the sound of the shots. I hurled myself forward, my feet slipping uncontrollably on the loose stones, and dived headlong into the black water.

I was out of my depth before I had covered ten yards. The salt water stung the numberless sore patches on my skin, but its welcome coolness was like a vitamin injection. My waterlogged clothes dragged me down, but not dangerously as yet; I didn't want to jettison them unless I had to. I trod water and looked back at the shore.

It was a dramatic sight. From my level, the whole hill-side was a solid wall of fire, turretted here and there with bright cones of flame. The trees that remained on the foreshore stood out in wavering silhouette, looking as insubstantial as a tracery in black lace. Their leaves were shrivelled, and their twisted shapes seemed to cringe and buckle as the fire reached for them.

Rick raced along the foreshore at the water's edge, his feet kicking up a diamond-dazzle of spray. I swam a little further out, then turned and watched him again. Something bumped softly against my legs: small fish, or bit of weed. I was no longer afraid of the gun. If he wasted time trying to shoot accurately at that range and in that uncertain light, he would never make it back to the boat. The fire was advancing too fast.

The same thought seemed to strike him at the same time. He hesitated, raised the gun, and lowered it again. He turned and began to run back the way he had come.

The heat seemed to be pushing him off the beach; all at once he was shin deep in water, and leaving a bow wave like a power-boat. He stumbled, waved his arms about in a frantic pantomime of alarm, and toppled sideways. Surprisingly, he made no effort to get up immediately, but stayed on all fours, groping all around him in the water. He had dropped the gun!

Something struck me hard on the shoulder, and I twisted round, yammering with fright. I had pushed the idea of sharks resolutely into the back of my mind, but in a flash the old terrors came crowding back in technicolour.

It was no shark, but my nerves were so strung up, that it took me a few seconds to recognize what it really was: a heavy, square-fronted scow, unmanned and drifting at the mercy of the current. It was about twelve feet long, and looked something like a small yacht-tender.

It was not difficult to visualize what had happened. The fire had eaten through the mooring-rope, and some quirk of wind or current had pulled the boat clear of the shore. I grabbed for the gunwale, and laboriously hauled myself aboard. Rick shouted something, but the words were unintelligible. I thought, with a glimmer of satisfaction : he wouldn't be using his voice, if he could use the gun. I

155

flopped onto the bottom boards, gasping like a landed fish. The luxury of allowing my limbs to relax was bliss, double-refined; I felt as if I would never want to move again.

Rick was still shouting. A new, shrill note of urgency in his voice penetrated my fuddled brain. I struggled to my knees and looked shorewards. He was waist deep in the water now, and the trees behind him were sprouting little buds of flame all over their trunks and branches, like freakish new growths. The wind was fluking in every direction, tousling the flames like unruly hair; a sudden blast of heat rolled out towards me, stinging my throat and squeezing tears from my eyes.

The force of the gust knocked Rick down again. His head disappeared under the water. He came up screaming; beating at the waves with his hand, in a childish panic.

'Here!' I tried to shout, but I could raise nothing better than a croak. 'Swim, you idiot!'

Wearily, I began to examine the craft for the first time. At the stern, the outboard motor was swivelled forward on its bracket, the screw out of the water. I tipped it upright and felt around for the starter-cord. It wasn't there. I had never encountered this kind of engine before. It would probably have a key-switch, or some kind of handle-starter gimmick. No doubt it was fantastically efficient, if only I understood it. As I fumbled around, cursing, Rick shouted again. 'Help me! Please, help me! For God's sake!' He was bleating with terror.

The current had carried me further away from him, and the boat was drifting sluggishly along a course roughly parallel to the shore, and about thirty yards out. Rick waded awkwardly along the beach, trying to keep level with me.

'I can't start the motor!' I rasped. 'Swim!'

I yanked on the tiller. The boat's head came round a few degrees, but we continued to drift sideways. I had to find some way to control her. There were no rowlocks, but to the left of the outboard-motor in the stern, was a

156

notch that looked like a sculling-port. The oar was held on clips under the wooden thwarts. The craft was heavy and cumbersome, and as reluctant to move as a broken-winded nag, but I got her headed for the shore at last. But by that time, we had drifted another five yards out, where the current seemed to be stronger. If I relaxed for a moment her head would wheel round like a hound following a new scent, and I had to fight her back on course. My last reserves of strength dwindled rapidly.

'Come *on*!' I shouted.

Rick shook his head violently, and mouthed something I couldn't catch.

'What?'

'Jellyfish!' He gesticulated wildly at the stretch of water between us.

I looked over the side. I had never seen jellyfish like these before, and I had never seen so many at one time. Uncountable thousands of huge white translucent balloons crowded the water. Some trembled, some tumbled over and over in slow motion; a few winked in the depths with a dull phosphorescence that was eerily sinister. I didn't know how dangerous they were, or even if they were dangerous at all; but their stealthy palpitation made my flesh creep.

The bow began to swing round again, and I went back to my sculling. The motion in the water sent the deathly-white balloons rolling and swirling in a lethargic, unearthly ballet. I felt sick, and my head reeled with exhaustion. Rick would have to make up his mind quickly, or my strength would give out completely. I coaxed more effort from my complaining muscles; the oar bounced in the port, and began to slide over the stern. I couldn't understand what was happening at first. I fell sideways and hit my head on the engine cowling. I could see two oars momentarily, but I didn't seem able to reach either of them. They floated parallel in the water and drifted out of reach. The boat rocked violently: water slopped over the side.

I found myself half-sitting, half-lying in a shallow puddle of water that sloshed gently from side to side. It was very soothing.

I raised myself up on one elbow and called out to Rick to hurry. He didn't seem to hear me. At least, he made no answer. He stood very still and straight, like a soldier at attention. I wanted to let him know that the oar had gone, that I couldn't control the boat any more; but my voice collapsed in a fit of feeble coughing. I beckoned to him as urgently as my flagging strength would allow. At last, as if he had been waiting for a signal, he launched himself forward, his arms windmilling like a madman.

Once he was well into the water, he was difficult to see against the firelight. His head was a bobbing black shadow on a moving patchwork of shadows. Hot ash blew into my face, blinding me temporarily. By the time I had knuckled my eyes clear, Rick had disappeared.

There had been no sound, no warning. He had just gone, as silently and undramatically as an ice-cube in a warm drink. I tried to locate the place where I had last seen him, but the boat wheeled in the current. and orientation was difficult. I felt frustrated, and vaguely angry: I'd missed seeing him die. And there were still questions I wanted to ask. I rested my head on the wooden thwart under the tiller, and wept.

The rain woke me. It fell in big soft, widely-spaced drops out of a jet-black sky. I couldn't see the fire any more, although its glare still purpled the low-flying clouds. There was no sign of Rick. I was alone in a black, wet, spongy void.

The rain grew heavier minute by minute. Soon it was pelting down so hard that it struck in a solid mass, like the jet from a hosepipe. It plastered my hair to my scalp and made rivers down each side of my nose. The glow from the fire faded fast; it was not likely to survive that deluge for long.

My mouth and tongue ached with thirst. I cupped my hands to the downpour and drank greedily. The puddle in the bottom of the boat deepened, and the ungainly craft settled more heavily in the water. I would have to find some way to bale her out if we were to stay afloat. Not for the first time that day, I was hardly master of my fate. I had lost the sculling-oar, I couldn't start the outboard motor, and I was lost in a thunderstorm. What's more, the boat was sinking.

The dinghy took the initiative by running aground. It bumped and grated along the pebbles and then tipped sideways at a drunken angle. Lightning streaked overhead with a sizzling sound, followed by a clap of thunder that nearly lifted me into the sodden air. The flash showed me that I was on the fringe of another rock-strewn beach, with trees almost down to the water's edge. I waded ashore, hunched my shoulders against the beating rain and waited for another lightning-flash to give me my bearings.

I didn't have to wait long. The sky growled and rattled and erupted into a continuous barrage of heavy artillery. The lurid glare showed me a harsh, unreal landscape in grey-and-black, blurred by the driving rain. It didn't seem to make much difference which way I went; I turned my back to the wind, and trudged along the beach.

I lost track of time; I had blundered into a world where time had no meaning. I staggered on, concentrating on the effort of putting one foot in front of the other. I seemed to get nowhere; every yard I covered was just like the one before and the one before that. I mumbled through old songs and half-remembered verses to keep my rubbery legs on the move; the beach stretched on, the rain hammered down, and the lightning made fancy sword-play in the heavens. Then, in a moment of rest from the endless, echoing drum-roll of the thunder, I heard a sound that brought me to a halt quivering like a gun-dog. It was clear, high, and totally unexpected: the frightened bleating of a sheep.

The sound came again; and this time it was answered

by a whole chorus of bleating, quavering down the scale from shrill treble to gravelly bass. And counterpointing that music was another melody: the unmistakable clank and rattle of railway goods-wagons.

The ground sloped sharply up from the beach; as I scrambled up the hill, the bushes deposited their accumulated load of rainwater on me, but my clothes had long since reached saturation point. I walked into something: a low, wire-mesh fence. The bush was cleared on the far side of it, and in the sputtering light of the storm, I saw the train quite clearly. It was emerging slowly from a cutting in the rock, and running towards the water along a raised embankment. There had to be a bridge there; it had been hidden from my view earlier by the curve of the headland.

I fell over the fence, and clawed my way up the embankment. I didn't know where the train was going, but it was going somewhere; and this neck of the woods had lost its attraction as far as I was concerned.

The carriages were tall, two-tier pens, packed to over-flowing with wet, smelly sheep. I couldn't see any way of hitching a lift. The pens were moving slowly, barely at walking-pace; and I watched with a growing sense of frustration as carriage after carriage rattled past. I had almost given up hope, when the last three carriages appeared. These cages were empty, their wide doors propped open. I heaved myself into the first one, and sprawled on the floor, resting my back against the rear wall. The floor was slimy, and the smell overpowering, but compared with flogging along a strange beach at night in a thunderstorm, it was pure luxury.

The lightning danced, and the electric glare showed me nothing beyond the grey rectangle of the open door but blackness and the slanting, steely rain. I was nowhere; floating between earth and sky with nothing for company but a concerto of primitive sound: hissing rain, thunder flapping like a loose sail, and the even, rhythmic clacking of the wheels.

The train picked up speed, rattled along busily for a while, and then slowed almost imperceptibly to a halt. There was some cheerful shouting up ahead, a prolonged gasp from the engine, and then complete silence.

I shuffled to the door and looked out. There wasn't much to see. A few wooden shacks and boathouses; an open space dotted with tall trees; a few sailing-dinghies grounded on a pebbled beach; and in the foreground, two small ferryboats moored each side of a wooden jetty. The rain had slackened visibly; the few street-lamps glittered like jewels in the washed air. Beyond the jetty, near a line of parked cars, a group of men stood, staring across the water and making desultory conversation.

I lowered myself to the track and limped towards them. Almost immediately I knew that I wasn't going to make it, my legs were abominably stiff and unwieldly; and waves of dizziness assaulted me at every step. The ground tilted at crazy angles under my feet.

Heads turned in my direction; a couple of men detached themselves from the group and started running. I think they intended to catch me before I fell, but I was too quick for them. I fainted before they had covered half the distance.

Chapter Eighteen

They revived me with brandy and shouts of encouragement, then battered me with questions. What had happened to my boat? Where had it gone down? Was anybody else on board? Had I been trapped by the storm or the fire, or both? I shook my head numbly, and mumbled replies. I don't know what I said, and I don't think they listened to much of it. They had one overriding interest: was anyone else in need of rescue? They repeated that question a hundred different ways, to make sure it penetrated my fuddled brain.

I told them about Rick Lucy. It didn't sound coherent, even to me, but they seemed to make some sense out of it. At least, it got them moving. A tall, skinny man took charge of the questioning: 'The last time you saw him, he jumped in the water to escape the fire?'

'Yes.'

'So we know roughly where he went in. You say you never saw him again?'

'That's right.'

'How long ago was this?'

'I don't know. Soon after the fire started.'

Another man comented: 'We got the alarm over two hours ago. Say two-and-a-half hours.'

'Right.' The skinny man considered. 'We'll take two boats, mine and Morrie's. Jack, you stay here in reserve; we'll maintain radio contact. Syd, you get on the blower and report to the C.A. After that, you'd better attend to

162

our chum here.'

Someone pushed his way to the front of the group. 'I'll take care of that, sir. I've met Mr Tallis before. I know where he lives.' The newcomer's face was in the shadow, but his unruly mop of hair glinted yellow in the lamplight. I had recognized the Northern twang in his voice.

'Ken Walters?'

'That's right sir.'

'What are you doing here?'

The skinny man cut in: 'Seeing as you two know each other, we'll get moving. That fellow may still be alive.' The group dispersed rapidly, fanning out along the beach and jog-trotting down to the boats.

Ken Walters set me on my feet and helped me walk up to the beach road. He opened the door of a battered old Volkswagen and gestured for me to get in. He still hadn't answered my question.

I hung back suspiciously; the day's events had soured my instincts. He answered my hesitation, as if I had spoken aloud. 'Bush fire alarm,' he explained patiently. 'I'm on the roster.'

I climbed stiffly into the passenger seat and Walters adjusted the seat-belt tightly round me. 'She's a little past her prime,' he said apologetically. 'But she's reliable.' He swung the Volks round in a tight arc, and we lurched over a level crossing. 'We'll be back in Sydney inside of an hour.'

The car was the first really dry place I had been in for some time. It made me uncomfortably aware of how wet I was. Water dripped off me everywhere. It squelched under my buttocks and ran down my legs to enlarge the puddle between my shoes.

Walters rummaged in his pockets. 'Are you hungry? I've got some chocolate in here somewhere. It'll restore some of your blood-sugar: lift your energy-level a bit.'

If anybody's energy-level needed a lift, it was mine. I seized the chocolate gratefully and bolted it like a starving sea-lion gulping down fish-scraps. Walters glanced at me approvingly: he liked to see me doing the right thing by my blood-sugar. 'No alcohol, I'm afraid.' He was reading my mind again. 'But I may have a little more chocolate.'

He rummaged some more, hampered slightly by his seat belt; and some papers and a small leather folder fell from his pocket. I picked them up for him, glanced idly at the folder, then studied it closely in the glow from the dashboard. It contained a good photograph of Walters, and a tersely-worded statement identifying him as a constable in the S.M.P. An embossed golden seal partially obliterated the signature at the bottom.

'You're a cop?' I asked. I really couldn't summon up any great feeling of surprise.

He nodded, and absent-mindedly ate some of the chocolate before passing the rest over. 'Thought you'd rumbled me back there. I was on Surveillance until I fouled it up two times in a row. We're not suppose to approach the subject except in an emergency. Every time I was on duty, there was some goddammed emergency.'

The storm was catching up with us again. Raindrops splattered against the windscreen like random bursts of buckshot. I began to feel jittery. 'Are you really trying to tell me that you were at that beach tonight by pure chance?'

'Not exactly.' He smiled. 'As a matter of fact, I thought I was going to have the melancholy task of organizing the search for your body.' The smile broadened into a grin. 'But happily, that assumption seems to have been as false as every other assumption we've made about you.'

'Look,' I growled, 'if there's one thing I can do without, right now, it's a cryptic cop.'

'Then I'll explain. At nine-twenty-eight last night, we picked up a known villain by the name of Paul Leslie Yapp, known to his associates as Polly. He was one of the men who attacked you the other morning, incidentally. Yapp was on the premises of the Starbird Motel when he was apprehended. In his possession at the time, were a key to your motel room, and a small-bore automatic pistol. The gun appears to have been the murder weapon used in the killing of Virginia Crewe in her beach-side home in Collaroy.'

We turned into a main highway just as the rain returned with a vengeance, swamping down so hard that the wipers could hardly deal with it. Barn-sized trucks swooped past, festooned with lights like fairground sideshows.

'This Yapp is a pretty tough character,' Walters continued, 'but when he realized he was carrying the can for a murder charge, he softened up considerably. He's been singing sweetly ever since. As a result of part of his information, a sizeable search-party was sent out to locate you. Or your body.'

'So where are you taking me now? To Inspector Bullock?'

'Of course. He may want to charge you with murder.'

'Whose?'

'Viriginia's.'

'But you copped Polly with the gun. It's obvious he was going to plant it in my room.'

'He doesn't deny it. What he says is, that he took it off you in the first place. Not all of the prints on the gun are his. Could they be yours?'

I brooded on this silently for a while. My prints were certainly on that gun; and Walters himself had seen me keeping watch on Virginia Crewe's house. The police might make an impressive case out of those two facts alone. Walters' voice cut across my thoughts. 'There's another thing,' he said casually. 'Did you kill Johnny Parvo?'

'No, he killed himself.'

'How do you know?'

'I saw him do it.'

Walters frowned. 'But you didn't report it?'

'No.'

'Mr Tallis, you don't need me to tell you that you're in a whole heap of trouble.'

'True. But I'll be in the clear as soon as they turn up that piece of film.'

'Film?' He became sharply attentive. 'What film is that?'

A truck thundered past like an express train, squirting out a bow wave of thin mud which obliterated our windscreen. The rain instantly washed it clear again.

I said tiredly, 'It's what the whole ball game is about. The film has evidence of a crime committed by Lucy, Parvo, and a man they call the Dancer. So far at least six people have died because of it.'

'Who's the Dancer?'

'I don't know.'

'Where's the film?'

'I don't know.'

'What happens if the film doesn't turn up?'

'Then I'm still in trouble.'

It was Walters' turn to brood. The rain drummed on the metal roof and flooded down the windows in horizontal waves. We were cut off in a hissing, rumbling, submarine world, haunted by the dazzle of oncoming headlights. After what seemed a long time, he said quietly, 'I see.' But he didn't specify what he saw. A moment later he added 'Got any ideas?'

'A vague hunch. Hardly amounts to a fully-fledged idea.'

'What is it?'

'It's too vague to talk about. Just something somebody said.'

'A possible lead to this film?'

'Barely possible. An outside chance.'

He considered. 'Want to give it a go? Right now? Maybe I can help?'

I shook my head. 'I'd need to do it alone. And I'd need my own car.'

'The yellow Lotus? That's about as inconspicuous as a fire engine, right now.'

166

'I know that.'

He thumped the wheel irritably. 'Mister, I can't just let you go off on your own. Not now. It's more than my job's worth.'

'Okay. You brought up the subject, not me.'

We had been cruising through the suburbs for some time now. Walters left the highway and picked his way through the deserted side-streets with easy familiarity. Suddenly he gave an exasperated grunt, pulled over to the kerb and killed the engine.

'How long would it take?' He turned to face me.

'An hour, maybe. Much less, if I'm wrong.'

'You're my responsibility, you see that? I wouldn't want you running out on me.'

'I won't do that.'

He started the car again. 'I must be out of my mind.'

We didn't speak again for the rest of the journey. Walters overshot the side-street where the Lotus was parked, and pulled in almost opposite Mick's house. Something seemed to be happening there: every light in the house was on, and a big official-looking car was sprawled carelessly across the driveway. I started across the road, hunching my shoulders against the torrential rain. Walters caught up with me and laid a warning hand on my arm. 'There's somebody watching us,' he said in a low voice. 'From the carport over there.'

I knew it was Diana, even before she moved out of the shadows. She was trying to crouch below the level of the dividing wall between the two houses, at a place where the car-port gave some shelter from the rain. I called her name; she began to run immediately, bolting diagonally across the neighbouring drive and into the street. She was carrying a black, square-cornered brief-case.

Walters recovered faster than I did. He vaulted over the wall with a daunting athleticism, and gave chase. I splashed along a few yards behind. Diana had kicked off her shoes for greater speed, but it was obvious that we were gaining on her. It was also obvious to me were she was heading. Suddenly she side-stepped into a narrow gap between two cars, and flung the brief-case at Walters' shins. He stumbled over it and crashed heavily into the bonnet of the nearest car. I skidded to a halt just in time to avoid falling on top of him. Diana, after one terror-stricken look behind her, sprinted across the street, and into the side-alley where I had parked the Lotus. I wondered whether she had visualized this sort of emergency, when she took possession of the car-keys.

By the time we had sorted ourselves out, Diana had disappeared around the corner. Ken Walters looked doubtfully at the brief-case, shrugged, and tucked it under his arm. He was noticeably slower after his fall, and limping a little. I raced ahead of him, trying to remember how far down the street I had parked the Lotus. Fifty yards, I thought: under a street-lamp.

I was right. I saw it as soon as I reached the corner. But the instant I saw it, it disintegrated into a million pieces, with a bang that broke every window in the street.

Chapter Nineteen

The blast threw me into the gutter and added a few more lacerations to my already ruined suit. The Lotus was just a charred, twisted heap of metal, and the street looked like a battlefield. Black smoke plumed from the wreckage, masking its grotesque outline; and for that I was grateful. I had no desire at all to see what was left of Diana.

Walters was unconscious. He lay face down on the pavement, still clutching the brief-case, which had burst open in the fall. A large, untidy pyramid of banknotes spilled out from the case, and was steadily flattened by the pelting rain. The notes were old, greasy, stained: eminently useable. They had been wadded into the case like old newspaper.

No-one had yet arrived on the scene, but someone had raised the alarm, somewhere. Sirens were hee-hawing in the distance.

I rolled Walters over. There was no sign of blood, and his pulse was beating strongly. He was wet through and lying in a puddle, but I didn't think he would come to much harm.

The sirens were getting closer: any minute now, the street would be full of curious, suspicious people. This was the last chance I was going to get. I took Walters' car-keys from his pocket, and ran to the Volkswagen. I was on the move before the first police car turned the corner.

At Milsom's Point, I looked briefly for Mick's car, but it

had gone from the spot where I had left it. I didn't waste time on the search. I swung the Volks onto the rutted dirt-track, and parked in the shadow of the old warehouse. I didn't think I had been followed, but I waited by the car for several minutes, looking first one way and then the other along the track. My clothes were filthy and water-logged, but I was so used to it by now, I hardly noticed. Lightning crackled somewhere on the far side of the hill. If anyone moved, I didn't see them.

I picked my way cautiously round the dark bulk of the warehouse. Visibility was poor down here; the only light came from the misty glare of the lamps on the street above. I found the loading platform and crouched underneath it, groping for the broken doors. There was a battered old suitcase covering the gap. I pushed it aside and poked my head into the darkness: 'Lucky?'

He was down there somewhere: I could smell him. He couldn't be dead drunk, I told myself; not on the fifty cents I had given him yesterday. But I had a horrible feeling I was wrong.

The blackness was oppressive. My heart began to pound, and my nerves jumped like fleas on a hotplate. My instincts told me I had made a fatal mistake somewhere, but I couldn't place it. The sound of tyres on the loose dirt put me wise. Like a fool, I had tried to play it too clever; and I had been outsmarted. Again. I grabbed the suitcase and ran, crouching and weaving, back to the car. As an im-provisation, it wasn't exactly inspired, but there was no time to think of anything better.

I yanked open the car door and threw the case onto the passenger seat. Something whined past my head. I didn't see where the shot came from, and I didn't stop to look. I didn't even try to shut the door. I had the car on the move before the second shot shattered the rear window and punched an untidy hole in the roof. I wondered what kind of gun he was using. At any rate, it wasn't that god-dam chopper. A small mercy.

The Volks bounced around on the uneven track like a pogo-stick on wheels, but the tyres and suspension survived somehow. I skidded onto the top road, and only just avoided a head-on collision with a white sports-car that was double-parked near the junction. It hadn't been there when I arrived. I would certainly have noticed it. It was Mick's car.

I didn't give myself time to think about that. Instinctively, I made for the main road. It was always crowded with traffic there, where the roads converged on the Harbour Bridge; and the crowds ought to offer some degree of protection. I was going to need all the help I could get, and soon.

The Volks was steering oddly, showing a tendency to swing towards the near kerb. The dirt track had been too much for the tyres, after all. Luckily, it was only a few hundred yards to the safety of the Bridge motorway.

When I got there, the road was deserted.

Wide, empty lanes glistened in the rain like polished metal ribbons, curving in a concrete landscape as bare of life as a science-fiction movie set. I hauled the Beetle into the centre lane, and tried to push the accelerator through the floor. I was more than half-way over the Bridge when I saw headlights behind me, coming up fast. At the same moment, the Volks gave a lurch, and the rear nearside wheel began to thump like a frightened jack-rabbit. I slowed down instinctively; I couldn't hold that speed with the tyre flapping like an old dish-rag.

And still there was no traffic. No sign of help anywhere. In the middle of the busiest part of the busiest city in the country.

As if it had been waiting for a cue, a red sports car rocketed towards me out of Clarence Street, like a front-runner at Brands Hatch. The headlights behind me were less than a hundred yards away. Without giving myself time to think about it, I swung the Volks right across the path of the oncoming car, and tramped on the throttle.

171

The red car swerved to my left, saw the headlights behind me, and pulled back again, brakes screaming like cats in agony.

It went past me sideways-on, its driver white-faced and mouthing obscenities. There was no crash, but both cars skidded to rest back to back and thoroughly stalled. The Volks limped half-way along the nearest side street, and stopped dead. A faithful servant can be pushed just so far and no further.

I got out and started running, taking the suitcase with me. It seemed sensible to get off the street as soon as possible. A flight of steps opened up on my right; I raced up them, and hugged the case to my chest as I slithered over the wet grass of a small park. I was in the shadow of the Bridge again, in territory that was familiar to me for some reason. I remembered the reason, and kept on running. I had a place to go to.

Somewhere over the Pacific, lightning flashed as regularly as a neon sign. I ran on without looking back. I didn't need to look back. He would be behind me somewhere; he had to be. Unless, of course, he guessed where I was going; in that case, he could drive round and be waiting for me when I arrived.

The theatre in Lomond Street was now guarded by a plank fence and boarded scaffolding. Notices along the fence warned off trespassers with the usual rubbish about guard dogs, but the crew hadn't even bothered to shut the double gates. Someone had left a tip-up truck parked in the entrance, its rear end sticking out a couple of feet over the pavement. I squeezed past the truck and looked hopefully into the cab, but for once the driver had remembered to take out the keys.

I paused for a moment to take my bearings. The truck was parked in the entrance of a long, narrow alleyway that ran down the right-hand side of the theatre. It was the only access-way to the scene-dock, at the far end; the only access-way to the theatre at all, apart from the foyer.

172

There was a huddle of machinery opposite the scene-dock doors: the big diesel generator, a couple of compressors. Half-way down the alley, a squat grab-crane stretched its ungainly neck over the ruins of a wall; and beyond it lay a wasteland of rubble and twisted steel. Mick had tackled the heart of the building first—the huge central shell of the auditorium. And he hadn't wasted any time. All that was left of it was the skeletal outline, in steel girders, of circle and balcony. At the other end, incongruously bracketing the still-elegant proscenium arch, the French rococco stage boxes drooped pathetically from the shattered masonry like gilt brooches on a drunken gypsy.

Plumb in the middle of this desolation, a yellow bulldozer perched on a mound of rubble that formed a shallow ramp down to the stage.

The rain had pounded the dust into a grey mud, that lay thinly over everything, and oozed in a sticky stream down the centre of the alley. There was only one place I could hide in: I stumbled over the wet and slimy rubble down to the stage area. At the bottom of the ramp, I tripped over a loop of rope, and fell heavily into a quagmire of mud. Under the mud, the wooden boards of the stage were still intact—demolition work was not even begun on this part of the building as yet. I waded upstage, carefully testing every step before putting weight on it, forcing myself to go slowly.

I had gone fully twenty yards before my outstretched fingers touched the back wall. Oddly, the mud here was deeper, in spite of the fact that the roof over the stage was still intact. Perhaps the subsidence had reversed the natural rake of the stage. If so, this part of the building was about as stable as a house of cards.

It was dark back here, but not dark enough. I was nowhere near safe yet. I was panting like a winded spaniel, and I thought all of Sydney must be able to hear the knocking of my heart against my ribs. I had made one mistake too many, and I knew it. The suitcase was my only hope,

173

and a frail one at that, since I didn't have the foggiest idea what I was going to do with it.

I could see nobody, hear no pursuit. The rain roared down relentlessly, and in the street beyond the tattered shell of the theatre foyer, a row of red lamps hung motionless, each light glittering wickedly at the centre of its own aura.

Minutes ticked by. The mud pulled softly at my shoes, and squelched at the slightest shift of weight. Nothing happened. Nothing moved. I began to be very afraid. This was worse than running. I edged along the wall, needing to keep on the move. I found a door. It moved a little way, but then the weight of the mud built up behind it, and it wouldn't budge further. The floor here seemed soft and spongy underfoot. I thought of that twenty-foot cellar under the stage, and clawed nervously at the wall for support. My hand struck metal. It was an iron ladder, bolted to the wall.

Holding the suitcase awkwardly under my arm, I started to climb. Anything was better than standing apprehensively in that clinging mud. The darkness was unnerving at first; after I had climbed only a few rungs I was completely disorientated. Curiously, the light improved a little as I got higher: I could make out the shape of some kind of platform to my right—a black smudge against the dark grey of the wall. The ladder came to an end; the platform was the only place to go. I crawled onto it, pushing the suitcase ahead of me. The ledge was gritty with brickdust and thickly strewn with coils of rope, planks and heavy slabs of metal.

The light was coming from a huge, lantern-shaped skylight in the roof, about thirty feet above me. It was masked from the stage itself by long black drapes, hanging at right-angles to the fly-grid. I wondered how long the drapes had been there: it had been years since the place had been used as a theatre.

I crawled the length of the platform, to the corner by

174

the proscenium arch. The electrician's box had stood here; there was even an old-fashiond dimmer panel, its rows of big iron wheels looking like a gigantic plate-rack. A few ropes still hung from the fly-grid; their ends had been bunched together and looped over the flimsy wooden guard-rail on the open side of the platform. I touched one of the ropes. It felt brittle in my hand, and as dry as a piece of wood. When I let it go, it slid over the rail and swung outwards with a rheumatic, creaking sound.

Almost immediately, a voice spoke out of the darkness. 'Thank you, Mr Tallis. I thought I knew where you were; now I'm sure.' He was whispering, and the cave-like echoes of the place gave his voice a sinister, disembodied quality. He continued smoothly, without waiting for an answer, as if he was demonstrating his ability to read my mind. 'No, I'm not bluffing. I really do know where you are. There!'

I ducked down out of sight behind the dimmer panel as the torchlight beam probed my corner. I couldn't tell whether he had seen me or not. He chuckled hollowly and switched off the torch. Now I knew where he was at least, but the knowledge was no comfort. The platform could only be reached by way of the metal ladder, and he was already climbing it. He was barely twenty yards away, and he had a gun. I had no doubt at all that he intended to use it.

'Walters?' I called softly.

The careful sounds of shoe-leather on metal stopped abruptly. 'So you guessed, Mr Tallis. What gave me away? My voice? Ever since I knew it was on record, I have gone to some pains to disguise it. I thought I managed rather well.'

'Well enough. It was the car that gave you away.'

'The car?'

'My car. You took me to it without asking directions. You had been there before.'

'Hardly conclusive?'

'It was enough for me, on top of all the other coincidences. And it explained why Diana was so terrified. She knew who you were. She must have seen you hanging about near the car earlier in the day; that's why she hadn't made her getaway.'

'Guesswork.' He sounded bored.

I lifted the suitcase, and moved stealthily to the guard rail. A fifteen-foot drop in pitch darkness wasn't inviting, but it offered better odds than facing the gun.

'One thing I can't figure out,' I said, 'is why they call you the Dancer.' I wanted to keep him talking as long as possible, but I was curious, too.

'Does it matter? The information won't help you.'

'Think of it as a last request.' I found the end of one of the ropes, slipped it through the handle of the suitcase, and knotted it swiftly.

'My real name is Waltzer,' he said off-handedly. He was on the move again, feeling around cautiously for the edge of the platform.

'American?'

'Yeah. I left the 'Nam in a hurry in '68. The nickname was Lucy's way of keeping me in line.'

'Blackmail?' I balanced the suitcase on the wooden rail.

'Let's say it ensured my loyalty.' He was clear of the ladder now. I pulled the slack of the rope clear of the rail. Any minute now, he would switch on the torch again, and—

Suddenly, the whole stage was filled with bright, glaring light. Huge floodlights above the proscenium arch sprang into life; and in the same moment I recognized the steady thumping of a diesel generator. I caught a glimpse of Walters' white, shocked face, and saw the muzzle of the gun swing upwards. Then I went over the rail in an ungainly dive, clinging for dear life to the suitcase and the rope.

It wasn't up to Tarzan standards, but what it lacked in grace, it made up for in speed. The sea of grey mud swept up to meet me, swept past my dangling feet. The rope

176

disintegrated on the return swing, but the mud and the suitcase cushioned my fall. I bounced to my feet and started floundering towards the auditorium. I thought I could hear shots, but none of them came near me. I must have made a difficult target anyway; I slid around on the slime like a clown in a banana-skin routine. The nearest cover was the left-hand stage box; I threw myself into it and ducked behind the ornate parapet.

Someone was shouting, over in the alleyway by the grab-crane. It was Bullock. Behind him, a broad white bandage round his head, was Mick.

'Keep down!' I yelled. 'He's got a gun!'

Mick waved and started running. I looked back towards the stage. Walters was swarming down the wall ladder like a monkey, the gun in his right hand. There was a heavy thump behind me; Mick had joined me in the box, breathing hard. Bullock was shouting again, something about the place being surrounded.

'It was me switched the floodlights on,' Mick muttered, by way of explanation. 'Is it the murthering bastard hisself?'

I nodded.

'He laid one across me nut then, the haythen. I'll skin 'um!'

'What's that Bullock is saying?' I panted. 'Is the place surrounded?'

'It is not.'

Bullock had advanced into the auditorium. 'This is the police!' he shouted. 'Put that gun away! There are police officers—'

Walters ran across the stage, shooting as he came. Bullock threw himself face down in the mud.

Mick watched the running man. 'Is it the suitcase he's after?'

'Yes.'

'Right.' Mick vaulted out of the box and ran to the middle of the auditorium. He climbed into the cab of the bulldozer and started to fiddle with the controls. He was the perfect target, if Walters looked his way. I stood up and lobbed a hunk of plaster at the stage. As a diversionary exercise, it was a waste of time. Walters wasn't paying attention to either of us. He was trying to free the suitcase from the rope. He looked cool, unhurried, as if he had taken the measure of the situation, and knew how to cope with it. He was outnumbered, but he still had the whip hand.

The roar of the bulldozer startled him, however. He pulled the rope free, and spun round to face the new menace, holding the suitcase in his left hand. Mick raised the blade of the bulldozer high, to give himself some protection. But he was still too exposed: he couldn't hope to manoeuvre the heavy machine quickly enough to avoid being outflanked. Walters took in the situation immediately. He watched the clumsy proceedings with undisguised contempt, as Mick pointed the 'dozer down the slope and opened the throttle. The big Irishman jounced around on the seat like a rodeo cowboy, shouting some savage Celtic war-cry. Walters stepped casually to one side, raised the gun and fired. Mick yelled and somersaulted off the back of the machine, which bore down relentlessly onto the stage. Walters moved to let it pass: he had brushed aside the whole futile attack with the aplomb of a chessmaster capturing a pawn.

He felt the danger rather than saw it, a split second too late. The rotten timbers of the stage, already loaded down with tons of mud, collapsed under the extra weight of the bulldozer. The section where Walters stood caved in abruptly. He tried to jump, still holding the suitcase, but the mud slid away under his feet, carrying him with it.

Unexpectedly, there was a huge splash: the under-stage cellar was flooded nearly up to floor level. Walters went under the brown, scummy surface, and came up still clinging to the case. The bulldozer teetered on the edge for a moment, its tracks still whirring, trying to pull itself up out of the morass; then it slowly slid back on top of him.

In the sudden silence, the lapping of the water seemed very loud. I became aware that the wall behind me was vibrating alarmingly. I jumped hurriedly out of the stage-box, and crossed the mound of rubble over the orchestra pit, where Mick was regarding the awesome crater with grim satisfaction. 'That side wall could go any minute,' he said calmly. 'Save the expense of fishing the bugger out to bury 'um.'

Bullock joined us, the rain making pink runnels in the mud on his face. 'What the bloody hell's going on?'

There were a few streaks of red on the brown surface of the water. Another section of the platform drooped, and a few splintered planks slid away.

'We've got to get that poor sod out of there,' Bullock muttered. He sounded as listless as I felt. 'Who was he? I never saw his face.'

'Rick Lucy's chief bogey-man,' I said numbly. 'They called him the Dancer. He was the one who killed Helen Simons.'

Bullock whistled and looked thoughtful. I asked: 'You knew him?'

'Only the name. He threw a long shadow. Everybody seemed terrified of him.'

'Yes.' I waited vainly for some sensation: triumph perhaps, or relief. Nothing. It was over. I was alive and he was dead. Helen was dead. I felt nothing at all.

'He was after the suitcase,' Mick said. 'He wanted that suitcase real bad.'

'Yes,' I said. 'Yes, he did.' The case still floated serenely on the muddy water.

Mick started forward. 'I'll get it before that bloody wall caves in.' He pulled it to the side of the stage with a spar of broken wood.

'What's in it?' Bullock grunted. 'Money?'

'No.'

'Dope? Stolen property?'

'No.'

'What then?'

'Take a look.'

Bullock heaved the case out of the water. Suspiciously, he snapped back the locks and lifted the lid.

'What the hell—' He stared at me angry-eyed. 'Some kind of joke?'

There were only two things in the case: a half-eaten sandwich, and a bag of peppermint candy.

'So Lucky did get himself something to eat,' I said.

'D'ye mean to say—' Mick scowled at the case as if it was a personal enemy—'that feller got himself killed for *that*?'

'I'm only sorry he never knew it,' I said. 'Come on, I'll show you what he was really after.'

Chapter Twenty

In fact, we didn't get away for three hours. Bullock insisted on getting Walters' body out of the flooded cellar before we left, and soon the theatre was crowded with uniformed police, firemen, and most of Mick's demolition gang. The place hadn't seen such a full house for decades.

Jimbo turned up, looking as laconic and unsurprised as ever. Without a word, he pushed me into the back seat of his car, and produced a flask of thick, sweet tea. My hand shook uncontrollably; I could hardly hold the cup. We sat there without speaking for a long time. The rain drummed on the roof of the car, the radio squawked, men squelched endlessly to and fro outside. There was a lot of shouting, but I couldn't distinguish any of the words. It's all over, I thought dully. It's all over, bar the shouting. The phrase went round and round senselessly in my brain, like a rat on the treadmill.

Bullock got into the front passenger seat, and slammed the door as if he was testing its strength. He had lost his bucolic look altogether; he looked tough and determined, and as mad as a hornet. He twisted round and glared fiercely at me. 'Talk!'

I talked. They listened impassively, neither prompting nor asking questions. Occasionally they glanced at each other with raised eyebrows and studiously blank expressions, but they offered no comment until I had plodded wearily to the end. As I talked, the dawn crept in, grey and cheerless; rain still bucketed down from the leaden clouds that

181

looked low enough to touch.

Still the officers kept silent, but the weight of their unspoken scepticism was as oppressive as the weather.

Finally, Jimbo sighed and looked sideways at Bullock. 'What do you think?'

'I think it stinks,' Bullock snapped.

Jimbo put on his excessively-bored voice. I had come to recognize that tone: it meant that his brain was clicking like a computer. 'Mr Tallis,' he drawled, 'you really are bad news. Even if every word you've just uttered is the living truth, you're the worst news around our backyard since Ned Kelly crossed the border. There's enough bloodshed and general mayhem on your file to send the whole of our judiciary into a decline.'

Bullock muttered something savage under his breath.

'And,' continued Jimbo smoothly, 'as my colleague has just intimated, you're the luckiest bastard God made. Not only have you survived in one piece, but your whole unlikely rigmarole has been corroborated by an unexpected accident.'

I stared at him heavy-eyed. 'I know,' I said. 'You picked up one Paul Leslie Yapp, otherwise known as Polly.'

Jimbo looked surprised. 'You knew that? No, Polly wasn't much help. The bonus was his associate, a young thug called Beverley Price, who happens, incidentally, to be a Catholic. We received an accident report on him about four hours ago: Price had apparently staggered out of the bush and stepped right into the path of a passing van. The van driver rushed him to hospital, the hospital authorities notified us, and an officer went round to investigate. Price was not seriously injured, but he believed he was dying from the effects of a snake-bite. He was distraught, hysterical. He kept moaning that he was in mortal sin and needed a priest. When the police officer arrived, Price evidently mistook him for the priest he had been begging for, and insisted on making a full and very interesting confession.'

'And the officer let him do it?'

'Our man swears—and this is corroborated by the nurse on duty—that he warned Price repeatedly of his mistake, but was ignored.'

'Why should you care?' Bullock asked sourly. 'It puts you in the clear.'

'More or less,' Jimbo shrugged. 'Could be tricky if this alleged film doesn't turn up.'

Someone shouted for Bullock, and he bustled off, slamming the door viciously again.

'The rain's easing,' Jimbo said. 'Sun'll be out by noon.'

'There's another explanation you owe me,' I said. 'How come Bullock and Mick Dooley turned up here just when they did?'

'No mystery about it. We were interested in Dooley because of his connection with the case—he was your friend, and he had been prying openly into Rick Lucy's affairs—but he was pretty stubborn about answering questions. Anyhow, when he was discharged from the hospital, Bullock offered to run him home—bit of softening up, you know? So Bullock was on hand when Mick discovered that his house had been broken into and his car stolen. Bullock phoned in a description of the car—it's quite an unusual make—and a patrolman spotted it almost immediately, at Milsom's Point. When they were driving over there, they heard on the car radio that there had been an explosion in the vicinity of Dooley's house, and that you had been seen in the area. So they got quite excited when you rattled past in that Volkswagen; they started to follow, but lost you before you reached the Bridge. Luckily, they came across the abandoned Volks, and Mick guessed that you were making for this place. Simple.'

Bullock came back. 'They got him out,' he said bluntly. 'Let's go.'

I had to argue with them for a long time before they would let me go down to the old warehouse alone. 'We'll be

183

watching you every inch of the way,' Bullock warned. 'Any funny stuff, and I'll crucify you.'

I was so tired, that the remark made me feel slightly hysterical. I stumbled down the path, giggling helplessly, the hot tears burning my cheeks.

The storm clouds were lifting and breaking up; wide gashes of blue sky showed through, dazzlingly bright. The rocks in the path were beginning to steam: in a few hours, the whole city would be like a Turkish Bath.

'Chuck?' I called. 'Chuck Starr?'

I was in luck. He was awake, and he was sober.

'Eh? Whatcher want?' Having found the cellar, Chuck had obviously adopted it as his home. He had arranged the heap of sailcloth into a passably comfortable couch, and shifted some of the other junk around, to give himself more space. Amazingly, it was quite dry down there.

Chuck Starr eyed me belligerently. 'Piss off!' he whispered. 'Bloody Commie!'

'I've come about the car, Chuck,' I said. 'Maybe we can do a deal. And I've brought your suitcase back.'

'What car?' he wheezed. 'I dunno what yer gassin' about. Who told yer me bloody name?'

'You did.'

'Not bloody likely. Never seen yer before in me life. Wouldn't forget a mouldy phizzog like yourn. Piss off!'

'You offered to sell me a car,' I said patiently.

'Never. What bloody car?'

'I'll give you twenty dollars to let me look at it. Ten now, and ten after.'

'Where would a bloody scruff like you get twenty dollars?'

It was a logical question. Compared with the way I looked, he was a model of elegance.

'Here.' I held out the money. 'It's a bit damp, but it's okay.'

He touched the notes gently with the tips of his fingers. 'There ain't no bloody car,' he said wistfully.

My heart sank. 'Come on,' I urged. 'I know all about it.

184

It belonged to the man who was hiding out in the house over there, didn't it? The man who was killed?'

The whites of his eyes showed briefly. 'You seen the corp, then? I didn't have nothin' to do with that, you know.'

'I know. But you saw him too, didn't you? You saw him before he was murdered, and you found his body in there. That's why you didn't kip down over there yourself. You saw that man hide his car somewhere; and nobody's claimed it since he died. That's the car you tried to sell to me.'

Chuck took the money and stowed it away inside his vest. 'Seein' as you know so much, you might as well know the lot. Give me a bunk up out of here.'

We didn't have far to go, but I would never have found it without help. On the harbour side of the cobbled yard, was a stone ramp leading to a small, box-like structure underneath the wooden jetty.

'In there?' I said. 'It's too small.'

'Bigger'n it looks. Used ter be a donkey-engine in there, an' stores. Nobody never comes here now. Bloody developers. 'Ow about the other five?'

I gave him the money. It was cheap at the price. In the glove compartment was a Hasselblad, worth about fifteen hundred dollars. The reels of film were in a plastic carrier-bag under the back seat.

Chapter Twenty-one

A dozen people volunteered at different times, to drive me out to the airport, but the trip had to be postponed so many times, a sense of anti-climax set in. Christmas came and went; I spent Christmas day alone in the motel, with the phone off the hook. The radio told me that the outside temperature had reached a hundred degrees, and there was good surf at Collaroy. After Christmas, the days passed somehow.

I didn't hear from Joybelle, but I read a news item about her. She had been interviewed on the Ron Blood Show, done a screen test for a local film company, and had been seen around with the lead singer of a visiting pop group. Her agent, Gillian, predicted a great future for her.

Mick called a few times, but we quickly ran out of conversation. The calls became less frequent as the weeks passed.

In the end, Jimbo was the only one who saw me off. I was glad; his cool, laconic style soothed my nerves. I longed to leave Australia: I felt imprisoned in a world where every stone, every tree, every dusty blade of grass brought Helen into my mind with a vividness that broke my heart a hundred times a day. She was part of this whole landscape, and my longing for her cast a melancholy over all of it. I had to get away. And yet—

'You've lost weight,' Jimbo said. 'You'll feel the cold in London.'

I didn't answer. I wondered what it would be like to

186

feel the cold. Would it numb my other feelings? We passed a brewery: its pungent smell filled the car.

'Of course, it's always possible we'll have to bring you back for the trial, if Lucy recovers.' Jimbo was making conversation.

'Is that likely?'

'Can't tell. The quacks are keeping him alive somehow. But they say if ever he comes out of the coma, his brain'll be gone. So maybe he won't stand trial anyway.'

We passed a golf-course; sweating men in shorts and brightly-coloured shirts dragged trolleys over clay-brown turf.

Jimbo made another effort. 'Helen Simons was an adopted child, did you know that?'

'No.'

'Abandoned by her parents as a month-old baby. Adopted eighteen months later. Real parents never traced. Heidi's parents on the other hand, were well known. Thieves and vagrants. Father died in prison. Mother died four years later, in hospital. It's just possible—' Jimbo hesitated— 'that they were sisters. It would explain the resemblance.'

'I suppose it would.'

'We finally traced Helen's foster-parents. It was a great shock to them. They were on a world cruise: that's why it took so long to find them.'

Jimbo helped me check-in my luggage, and walked with me through the airport's main concourse and out onto the observation platform. The air was sweet and cool; the sun as gentle as an English summer. It was a rare, perfect day; below us, in the loading bays, the aircraft sparkled like shiny toys. Three clouds hung in perfect formation in the blue sky. Jimbo started to say something, but I shook my head.

'It doesn't matter,' I said.

'No.' Abruptly, he shook my hand. 'I'll be off. Come back soon.'

'I don't think so.'

187

'Ah, well.' He turned and walked back to the concourse. At the gate, he raised a hand in salute. 'Stay cool.'

The three dark clouds hung in line over the silver dazzle of Botany Bay, unmoving, indifferent as the postcard-blue sky. I watched them until my flight was called. They didn't move at all.

If you have enjoyed this book and would like to receive details of other Walker mystery titles, please write to:

Mystery Editor
Walker and Company
720 Fifth Avenue
New York, NY 10019